AXE TO GRIND
A DCI PILGRIM THRILLER
Book 1

By
A L Fraine

The book is Copyright © to Andrew Dobell, Creative Edge Studios Ltd, 2019.
No part of this book may be reproduced without prior permission of the
copyright holder.

All locations, events, and characters within this book are either fictitious, or
have been fictionalised for the purposes of this book.

Book List

www.alfraineauthor.co.uk/books

Acknowledgements

Thank you to my wife Louise for her tireless support, my kids for being amazing, and my family for believing in me.

Thank you to my amazing editor Hanna Elizabeth for her critical eye and suggestions, they're always on point.

Thank you to my fellow authors for their continued inspiration.

And finally, thank you to you, the readers, for reading my crazy stories.

Table of Contents

Book List 2
Acknowledgements 2
Table of Contents 3
1 4
2 9
3 16
4 20
5 28
6 31
7 36
8 41
9 47
10 51
11 53
12 58
13 61
14 65
15 69
16 72
17 76
18 82
19 86
20 91
21 95
22 101
23 105
24 106
25 110
26 114
27 118
28 126
Author Note 129

1

"Oh, just shut up! I might as well be dead for all you care!"

Slamming the door behind her, Harper strode out onto the street and turned left. She made a point of not looking back at the house, just in case her mother was watching her through the window. She didn't want to give her the satisfaction.

She pulled her jacket a little closer, stuffing her hands in the pockets to protect them against the cool evening air.

The streets were already descending into darkness, lit by the sickly glow from the street lamps as they flickered into life. The occasional car drove past, but there weren't many people out and about tonight. Just a couple of cars and a van parked up the road. But that suited her just fine.

She wanted to be alone anyway. She needed some time with her thoughts, time to think things through and decide what she wanted to do.

As she pounded the concrete, not really thinking about where she was going and letting her feet go where they would, she sighed. After everything she'd been through, she'd come back here, to her mother's. All she'd wanted was some comfort, and maybe a little understanding, but clearly, that had been too much to ask for.

Instead, she just got judgement and a bloody lecture—something she really did not need right now.

Shaking her head, she realised she probably should have known better. When had her mum ever taken her side on things or backed her up? She was forever judging her and making her feel bad.

Maybe this had been a mistake.

A mistake! Ha. She smirked. Her whole bloody life seemed to be one mistake after another right now, and it looked like Seth might be the latest lousy choice.

What a pissing idiot. How dare he treat her like that. She'd hoped that, out of everyone, her mother would have understood her boyfriend troubles. But no, she took it as another opportunity to berate her and make her feel bad.

Freaking typical.

It wasn't as if her mother had a leg to stand on in that regard either. Her love life was an unmitigated disaster which had eventually left her bitter and alone. It was one of the reasons that Harper had moved out in the first place. When her father left, it hadn't taken long before Harper realised she needed to get away from her mum.

She'd never really approved of Seth, but Harper didn't see what business it was of her mother's, who she spent her time with. Getting a lecture on that from her mother was the height of hypocrisy as far as she was concerned.

In anger, she kicked a stone into the hedgerow beside her.

Why couldn't she just be nice? All she had to do was hug her, say a few nice things, and not get all high and mighty.

Was that so difficult?

Apparently.

Coming to a stop at a junction, Harper looked along the various branching roads, and decided to head towards town. She wasn't far from Epsom Town Centre, and she wondered if it would be busy. Part of her wanted to go and get a drink, maybe find someone she could hook up with for the night. That would serve Seth right for what he'd done to her.

As she contemplated her route, a shiver passed up her spine, and on instinct, she turned, looking behind her, half-expecting to see someone.

It felt like she was being watched, but she couldn't see anyone.

As she was about to dismiss it, she remembered having felt the same sensation a few times these last few days. Was it related, or was she finally going mad? Thinking back to Seth, and what he'd done, she figured that it wasn't unexpected that she should feel a little jumpy.

Was Seth out there somewhere, watching her, following her?

Well, screw him! I'll give him something to watch, she thought striding towards town.

Where the hell did he get off being so horrible to her? It wasn't right, and she wouldn't put up with it. As she stormed along the pavement, her head down and her jacket pulled tight, a car slowed as it passed her.

"Oi, oi!" someone shouted to her. "What's a pretty thing like you doing out here then, aye?" It was followed by a wolf-whistle.

Harper rolled her eyes and caught a glimpse of the car rolling past her with a leering man leaning out of the passenger-side window. She made a point of not looking at him and put up some mental shutters as she pretended she wasn't being cat-called.

"Give us a smile love, it can't be that bad," the man shouted.

Piss off, she thought. Where the hell did these idiots get off thinking that she owed them a smile or any kind of friendly gesture?

"Forget her," another voice from the car called out. "She's clearly a frigid bitch."

Laughter broke out in the car as it accelerated away. Looking up, she pulled a hand from her pocket and gave them the finger.

Bastards.

Closing in on the town centre, she started to see other people walking about in small groups, laughing and joking.

Their jovial attitudes and smiles irritated her. She didn't want to see that. Maybe this wasn't such a good idea.

Going into one of these bars and being surrounded by loads of happy faces sounded like hell to her, so she veered off, feeling like she had her own personal little black cloud following her around.

In her back pocket, her phone vibrated. Pulling it out, she saw the word 'Mum' glowing brightly in the night as the device buzzed again.

She did not want to talk to her right now.

Swiping the answer icon away, she cancelled the call before stuffing it back into her pocket. Maybe she should go and see a friend?

Maybe Vicky would help her... But the thought died just as quickly as it appeared. Vicky always seemed to take Seth's side in things. She'd be no help.

Walking further up the road, she started to pass a park and briefly considered going through it, but then that sinking feeling returned, as if there were hidden eyes in the darkness, watching her, following her.

Her phone buzzed once in her back pocket. For a moment, she thought about ignoring it, but the feeling of being watched made her long to be home again, inside, somewhere safe.

She pulled her mobile from her pocket and placed her finger against the fingerprint reader, bringing the device to life.

"I'm sorry," her mum had written. "Come home, let's talk. I'll just listen. Promise."

Harper sighed and suddenly felt terrible that she'd stormed out. Her mother only wanted the best for her. That's all she wanted. She knew that, and yet, there was no one else on earth who could push her buttons as well as her mother could. She just had a funny way of expressing herself, she guessed.

Looking into the grim darkness of the park, and the shadowed branches against the inky blue sky, she knew where she'd rather be.

She'd give her one more chance.

Crossing the road, Harper set off back in the direction of her mother's house, leaving the feeling of being watched behind as she wondered what would happen when she walked back into the house.

Would she listen? Would she hold back from expressing her unsolicited opinions about her life choices?

Only time would tell.

She'd just have to put up with any unwanted comments.

As she walked up the street, she noticed the side door of a white van on her left had been left wide open with no one was in sight. The darkness inside it hid whatever secrets it held, so Harper gave it a wide berth.

As she passed it a shadow shifted. Sudden movement off to her right caught her attention. Something grabbed her. An arm wrapped around her neck as a hand clamped over her mouth.

She could hear the man—she was sure it was a man—grunt from the effort of holding onto her. Harper struggled as he hauled her into the van. She clawed at the arm and hand as she fought for breath. Kicked wildly as the world around her begin to pull away. The street she'd been stood on seemed distant. Darkness crept in. Her vision tunnelled. Until it finally slipped away as she descended into nothingness. The last thing she heard before oblivion took her was the van's side door rolling shut, ending with a final slam.

When she started to come to, she found herself sat on a chair in a shadowy room. Her wrists hurt. She tried to move, but couldn't. She seemed attached to the chair, and it went with her whenever she tried to get up.

"Wha…?" She shook her head, fighting to bring herself out of the funk her mind was still mired in. She needed to be alert and sharp. "What the hell?"

She wasn't alone. She saw feet ahead of her and sat back with a jerk, nearly tipping the chair over. "Shit."

A man stood before her in a hoody with something covering part of his face. She couldn't make out any details. Who was he? It was so dark.

Did she know this man?

"What the hell? Let me out of here. What are you doing?"

The man didn't answer, but shifted his pose, revealing a large pair of bolt cutters hanging from his right hand. Harper's breath caught in her throat as she stared at the cutting edges at the end of the tool. She felt sick.

"What... What do you want? Money? What? We can talk about this. I can help you. Please."

The man didn't reply, he just cocked his head sideways slightly, as if he didn't understand her, or was maybe mulling over what she'd said.

"Please. I'll do anything. You can do whatever you like, just please, don't hurt me. Let me go, I won't tell anyone, I promise."

She heard a buzzing noise and looked over to see her phone on the floor nearby, beside her purse. It was her mother calling her again. She was probably wondering where she was.

"Mum..." she whimpered, choking back a lump in her throat. "Please, don't hurt me. Just let me go. I'll do whatever you want. Please."

A sob racked her body as the phone stopped buzzing. She looked at it longingly, but it was silent.

She turned back to the man. Pain exploded across her face as his fist caught her on the cheek and nose. It felt like she'd been hit by a brick or something. Had she cried out or yelped? Probably, but she couldn't really remember. The man was behind her now. She jumped as she felt him grab her right hand.

"No, please. Stop," she said, flexing her fingers and trying to slip her hand from his. He tried to manoeuvre her hand again, but she struggled and frustrated his attempts.

Something hard hit her in the side of the head. Lights burst in her vision, and she felt sure he'd just caved her head in. For a few moments, she felt dazed and had trouble focusing.

He was doing something behind her, but it took her a few moments to work out what it was.

She could feel something cold gripping the little finger on her right hand. Something hard, unyielding, and...Oh, God.

The man grunted. Pain bloomed and Harper screamed as he closed the bolt cutters on her finger.

2

"Jon."

He could see her, off in the distance, moving into the fog, not much more than a shadow, running towards the light.

"Charlotte, wait!" he called out to her. But she kept going. He ran, but it felt like he was running through treacle. The very world was holding him back.

"Jon?"

"Charlotte!"

She was so far off. He just couldn't get close. He'd never reach her.

"Jon!" The voice was right by his ear. Close. He turned. She was right there, right behind him. Blood fell in runnels over her face as she stared at him with dead eyes. "Save me, Jon."

An ear-splitting buzz shattered the dream, and Jon sat bolt upright in bed. Light spilt through the thin hotel drapes, lighting the room with a golden haze.

Grunting, Jon swung his legs over the side of the bed and tapped his phone, turning the alarm off. He thought back to the dream, which was slowly fading. Her face receded into darkness, pulling away from him, returning to memory. That's where she lived now, apart from on those odd nights when she'd intrude on his dreams, reminding him of the reasons for doing what he did. Reminding him of his mission.

"I'm sorry, Charlotte," he muttered. "I can't save you, but I can save others."

Jon rubbed his face with his hands and yawned. It was early, but he was keen to be on time—no need to make a bad impression on the first day.

Standing up, he moved to the curtains and pulled them wide, letting the light into the room as he looked out over the hotel car park and the Surrey countryside beyond.

"What the hell are you doing down here, Jon?" he muttered shaking his head. Now that he was here, and just hours away from his first day on his new team, he wasn't sure if he'd done the right thing.

First day nerves, he guessed. He felt sure he'd get over it soon enough. Running his hand through his hair, he stumbled through the room like a zombie, stubbing his toe on the bed, before eventually finding his way into the shower. Afterwards, feeling just a little more like one of the living, he got dressed as he watched the local news.

"Yesterday saw the continuation of the Devlin case, during which Mr Devlin's wife, Faye, made an appearance with her son and spoke with the press outside the Guildford courthouse," the news anchor said, as the visuals cut to footage.

"This is a setup," the woman on the screen ranted. Abban is a good man! He'd never do what they say he did. It's because he's Irish, isn't it? That's what it is."

"Mother, please, not now," her son said, trying to pull her away from the cameras as she held up her hand in a V-for-victory sign.

"My husband is innocent! It's that Terry Sims that did it, not Abban. I know it."

"If he's as crazy as you are, love…" Jon commented with a wry smile while he finished dressing and then made his way downstairs. There was no way he was missing the complimentary breakfast that came with the room hire.

Everything was so bloody expensive down here, he was keen to get the most out of everything.

The breakfast was pretty good, although there was no black pudding to go with the otherwise top drawer Full English. He felt quite sure that he could get used to that every morning and felt doubly sure that his waistline would never forgive him for it.

Feeling satisfied and full, he was soon on the road in his Vauxhall Astra, heading east out of Guildford. He'd driven past Horsley Station yesterday to make sure he knew where it was, and backtracked his way over there, navigating through the morning traffic that was mostly heading into the city. He felt glad he was heading away from Guilford, judging by the lines of cars that were queuing on the other side of the road.

He was early but thought it right that he started as he meant to go on, and wanted to show the officers that would be working under his command what he would expect from them.

The countryside around here was leafy, green, and in places, reminded Jon of Nottinghamshire. There wasn't much else to remind him of home, though. It was in many ways, a world away from the life he'd known.

He'd already seen countless large houses. Mansions really. Huge places with gated entrances and fountains in the driveway between collections of gleaming cars.

It was sickening to see such wealth on display, but then, he guessed that was Surrey. Commuter belt. Home of the wealthy and the famous. But also, strangely, the home of a unit of officers with a very specific mission.

He was keen to get into the office and find out a little more about them and the people he would be working with. It was the unit's focus that had caught his attention. Mainly because it was the same goal that he'd personally chosen five years ago, and he was keen to see where it might take him.

He'd done as much as he could with the CID team in Nottingham and knew he'd pushed his superiors as far as they were willing to bend. They'd warned him about his obsession, and how it was starting to damage the unit. He'd done his best to hide his continuing quest, but it was just a matter of time before he went too far.

Damon's call had come at just the right time, it seemed. It was almost serendipitous. Moving away from Nottingham had been hard. Leaving behind everything that he knew, and the few friends that he still had to take this job had not been easy. Not least of which because it meant him leaving behind a place that was filled with so many memories, including his memories with Charlotte.

But, there was no grave to visit, just a small plaque on a wall somewhere that he'd never visited. She lived inside him now. Just a memory that he carried with him. He had to keep reminding himself that it really didn't matter where he was, she would always be with him.

When Damon had explained why he wanted him, why he'd thought of him, it all seemed to fit into place. He'd taken his time, thought it through and tried to think what Charlotte would want for him.

But he didn't need to think. Not really. He knew the answer. He knew what she'd want him to do.

So he took the job.

Driving into the small, leafy village of Horsley, the large, brutalist building on the right-hand side of the road stood out like a sore thumb. The station rose from the surrounding countryside to loom over the road like a cinder block in a carefully manicured rockery.

And yet, it radiated strength and power, sending an unambiguous message to the criminal fraternity that permeated all walks of life, no matter how rich or poor they were. It looked fairly new too and promised to house good facilities for the unit to use.

He pulled in and parked up, taking one of the visitor spaces at the front. Once he'd received his ID card, he'd park around the back, but for now, this would do.

Climbing out, Jon looked up at the concrete edifice and took a breath before he marched inside and approached the front desk.

"DCI Jon Pilgrim, I'm here to see Damon Verner."

"That's Inspector Verner to you."

Jon turned to the voice and saw his old friend walking into the reception through a security door.

"Damon, good to see you," Jon said in greeting. He smiled. "You look… well, I would say good, but that would mean me being nice to you."

"I see you haven't changed at all, Pilgrim," Damon replied shaking Jon's hand, before pulling him in for a brief embrace that consisted of a lot of back-slapping, and precious little tenderness. "Seriously, it's good to see you. I'm glad you could make it down."

Damon was a good deal shorter than he was, with thinning, slicked-back hair and circular glasses that pinched his nose and reminded Jon of a mole.

"No problem. Happy to help. Sounds like you've got quite the operation going on here."

Damon nodded. "Yeah, we do. It's been great. It should be right up your alley."

"You stay away from my alley," Jon replied with a wink. "So, you're NCA now? Moving up in the world."

"What can I say?" Damon shrugged. "They recognised my expertise."

"Are you sure that's what it was? They didn't just want to get you off the streets?"

"Yeah, maybe," he replied with a wry smile. "How are you, Jon?" His tone was serious, and Jon knew what he was getting at. "Are you okay?"

He nodded. "Yeah, I'm fine, don't worry about me. That was all a long time ago now. Your offer came at just the right time—I think I've pissed off enough people up north. Figured I'd better expand my horizons and see how many I could annoy down here too."

"I think you'll find that your dedication to the cause will serve you in good stead."

"That would be a turn up for the books," he answered, and signed in where the receptionist indicated. She handed him a temporary ID card.

"I'll get you a proper one of those," Damon commented.

"Good, I don't want to look like the work-experience guy all day."

"Come on, this way," Damon said, and led him through the door he'd first appeared through, unlocking it with the ID card that hung around his neck.

"So, tell me a little more about this unit," Jon asked, admiring the clean halls and modern décor. It had a fresh, simplistic style to it that Jon kind of liked.

"The SIU is a unit dedicated to taking on some of the most notorious and vicious cases in the UK."

"So, serial killers?"

"Yes, but not just them. Our remit is much bigger than that. We'll talk a little more upstairs. The Chief Superintendent is keen to meet you and get you up to speed as quickly as possible."

"What's his name?"

"Collins. Darrell Collins. He's alright, you'll like him."

Jon nodded. Liking him wasn't really all that important. What was important was if the chief would let him do his job in the way he needed to. But, if he was someone he could get a pint with as well, then that would be great, too.

They reached the top of the stairs and approached another set of doors with another security lock. While Damon moved to unlock them, Jon eyed the sign beside the door.

SOS-SIU.

Jon raised an eyebrow at it and peered at the words below, that explained the acronym. Serious, Organised, and Serial – Special Investigations Unit.

"Really?" Jon muttered.

"Hmm? What?"

"SOS? That's a bit on the nose, isn't it?"

"Oh. Heh, yeah, maybe."

Jon eyed him and noted the flush of colour that filled his cheeks. "Did you come up with that?"

"Well…"

"I knew it. You sly dog."

"I like it."

"I bet you do. Jesus," Jon muttered, shaking his head. "Stick to your day job, Damon."

"Right, come on, let's not keep him waiting."

"I'm early, man."

"So's he," Damon replied, looking back at him with a knowing smile.

"Aaah, one of those, is he?" he replied, already getting an idea about what the chief was like, and approving of it.

"When he knows we have someone important coming in."

"Flattery will get you everywhere," Jon commented as he followed Damon through a large open-plan office space with incident rooms, meeting rooms, and offices around the edges. Several men and woman stopped whatever they'd been doing and watched as they walked through the room. Jon smiled at them but didn't linger.

Damon led Jon into what looked like the main meeting room, complete with a long table down the middle. Sat in one of the chairs, with a leather folder open before him was a grey-haired man, who turned keen eyes on Jon.

"One moment," the chief said, returning his attention to his work and making a couple of final notes before closing it and turning to face him. The chief superintendent sat back in his chair and regarded Jon with appraising eyes. "DCI Jon Pilgrim. I'm Chief Superintendent Collins. Damon speaks highly of you, Jon."

"That would be a first," Jon replied, unable to help himself, but also keen to test the waters. He wanted to see how the chief would react to his comment.

Damon gave him a look, and the chief raised an eyebrow. "A joker, then."

Jon shrugged. "Occasionally. Sorry, nice to meet you, sir. Thank you for the opportunity."

"You have Damon here to thank for that. You were the first person he suggested."

"I'm honoured."

"You should be," the chief replied regarding him for a moment before pulling a piece of paper from his folder and looking it over. "You have an exemplary arrest record, DCI Pilgrim."

"Thanks. I do my best to make a difference."

"Admirable. You seem to like taking on the vicious ones. The murderers and such."

"I have been making that my focus, yes." In his mind, Charlotte's face flashed before his eyes, along with many of the troubling memories of her final moments on this earth.

"I see that. It seems to have defined your policing over the last few years."

"Yes, sir."

"Good. Alright, well, I'm glad to have you here, so let's bring you up to speed. The SIU was formed recently in response to a series of killings in the area, and the need to have a dedicated team that was designed to handle some of the more… complex cases. Formed in partnership with the National Crime Agency, our team operates throughout South East England, and could, in theory, go even further afield. We take on serial killers, organised groups, and other serious and vicious crimes."

"So, like the Met's Flying Squad, but for murderers rather than robbers," Jon replied.

"Something like that, yes," the chief replied. "As a new group, formed from a Surrey Murder Team, we're still building up our numbers. We have a central core team of officers, supported by other specialists, and of course, the wider Police forces in Surrey and beyond. We were missing a DCI, however, and I felt it important that we filled that role as soon as possible. That's when Damon recommended you."

Jon nodded as the chief explained the situation, adding to the information that Damon had already given him. "I understand, sir."

"Good. Well, I'm very much looking forward to seeing how you do here. I'm expecting good things from you, Jon."

"I'll try not to let you down, sir."

"Good man," the chief replied, standing up and slapping him on the shoulder. "Good man. I'll be upstairs in my office if you need me. In the meantime, why don't you introduce him to his team?" he said to Damon.

"Sir," Damon replied.

With a final nod, the chief walked out, leaving the two of them alone.

"I think that went well," Jon commented.

"About as well as I expected it to," Damon replied sarcastically.

"You're just jealous of my razor-sharp wit," Jon commented.

"Yeah, that's right, that's what it is," he answered unconvincingly, as he made for the door. "Come on, let me introduce you to the lucky people you'll be working with."

"Lead on," Jon replied and followed Damon out of the meeting room and back into the main office where he approached a group of five people sat and stood around in a group, talking.

"Everyone, thanks for getting in promptly this morning. I want to introduce you to your new DCI, Jon Pilgrim."

Jon nodded and smiled, looking each of them over.

"Jon," said a messy-haired man, wearing a shirt that looked like it could do with an iron. He stepped forward and offered his hand. "DI Nathan Halliwell."

Jon took his hand with a firm grip and shook it. "Nice to meet you, Detective Halliwell."

"And you," Nathan replied. "This is DC Faith Evanson, our Victim Support Officer, DC Dion Dyer, DS Rachel Arthur, and DS Kate O'Connell."

"Mornin'," he said in reply, smiling at them, wondering what kind of officers they were. There were several younger looking ones amongst them, and he hoped they would be as dedicated to the job as he was.

Kate stepped forward and offered her hand too. "Good to meet you," she said with a smile. She was a striking woman wearing a fitted suit with her auburn hair tied back in a ponytail.

"And you," he replied. He enjoyed sharing her gaze for a moment before he pulled his eyes away and looked around the office. In his mind's eye, Charlotte was watching him, and he felt guilty for looking at another woman in that way. "Nice place you have here."

"It's not bad," Nathan replied, sounding a little less than enthused.

"Ignore him," Kate cut in. "It's pretty good, actually. We've got some great facilities, including a small forensics suite, cells, even a gym in the basement."

"Wow," Jon replied, genuinely impressed. He wondered if some of the money sloshing around this county had actually gone towards a good cause for once. "Fancy."

"It was built as business premises, but the company that was constructing it went bust. So a local businessman bought it and donated it to the police."

Jon nodded his approval. So, it seemed he was right in his assumptions. But he couldn't help but wonder if this was some kind of tax write-off for the local philanthropist. He didn't know many wealthy people that would do such a selfless and expensive thing.

"You've got it good here," Jon said, looking over at Kate.

"It's been good to me so far," she answered. "I hope you like it."

He nodded, feeling buoyed by the people and facilities he'd seen so far. This could be exactly what he needed.

3

Alan turned off the main road onto the track, before pulling up behind the familiar car that was parked up to one side.

Brutus barked once in the boot, clearly excited for another day at work.

"Yes, yes, we're here," Alan said as he climbed out and moved around to the back of the car. Inside, Brutus watched him, his tail going as he waited. Alan opened the boot and pulled Brutus in for a hug, running his hands through his fur.

"Good boy, who's a good boy, huh?" Attaching the lead, Alan led him from the back of the car and up the cracked concrete track to the prefab security station on the left. Beyond it, large metal gates blocked the road, denying the curious entry into the site beyond.

Alan walked into the security station to find Dave sat with his feet up and his hands behind his head. "Mornin'. Busy night, was it?"

"Nah, quiet actually," Dave replied as he let Brutus off the lead. The huge Alsatian loped over to Max in the corner, and the two dogs greeted each other excitedly.

"Good. Hopefully, mine will be as uneventful. I'm getting fed up of chasing bloody pikeys off this site."

"I hear they're moving up the demolition date, I doubt we'll be here for too much longer."

"That would be nice."

"Brutus clearly likes it though."

"Heh, yeah. He loves it. Gets him out and about, what's not to love?"

"Everyone alright at home? How's the missus?"

"Yeah, she's alright. We're not doing much, really. Just the usual, you know?"

"Oh, sure. I know. Just life stuff. Right then, Max, we've got to go."

Alan looked over at the two dogs who were now laid side by side on the doggy duvet, watching them. Max's ears pricked up at the sound of his name. Dave got up and urged Max to follow with a slap of his thigh. Max grabbed his squeaky toy, bounded up to Dave, and followed him out.

"Have a good one, matey."

"Will do," Alan replied, and settled into the seat beside the main computer. He'd go through his usual routine, checking his email and any work messages before taking a walk through the site to check it out.

As usual, his inbox was filled with junk, scams, and promotional rubbish with precious little of interest in it at all. Still, he went through it and started to read up on some work messages.

He was less than an hour into his shift when the alarm control panel in the PC lit up.

"Really?" Alan muttered, eyeing the program and the alert from the onsite passive infrared sensor. "They're in early today," he muttered, glancing at the time.

He watched and waited for a moment, wondering if they'd set off another PIR alarm. He knew which one had triggered, and it did have a habit of going off all by itself occasionally. Or maybe it was a fox or something. But, sure enough, a second one lit up a short time later, making the odds of it being an animal, much smaller.

"Shit," he cursed and got up. "Looks like we're heading out early, B."

Brutus sat up, alert and ready. "Come on, let's go and scare some idiots," he said and got the dog on a lead before walking out of the cabin.

The change in Brutus as they made their way through the gate and down into the site was always impressive. The dog knew when they were working and immediately got his game face on, his head sweeping left and right, sniffing the air as Alan wandered in. He moved slowly down the short lane, keeping quiet and listening out for voices and sounds of movement. On reaching the end of the lane, the whole site opened up before him. Several large buildings were clustered together, including a couple of warehouses, the main factory, and off to one side, the offices. The derelict building sported exposed metal beams, smashed windows, and some admittedly impressive graffiti.

Alan knew where the sensor was that had been tripped. He made a slow circle of the building towards the entrance that he believed had been breached.

Partway around, after seeing and hearing nothing, a sudden, blood-curdling scream rang out from inside. The terrifying sound brought Alan up short, making him pause. It had sounded female. Frantic shouts and the clatter of several sets of feet followed.

What on earth was going on?

Alan pressed on as Brutus started to pull on the lead, eager for action. Moving at a quicker pace, and catching the occasional shout from inside the building, Alan rounded the corner and approached the open loading dock where the PIR had been triggered. He was about to turn into it when four teenagers came crashing out through the door. Three male and one female, they were essentially kids, and they looked terrified. Several of them were shaking and looked in a state of shock. Alan held Brutus back as he pulled on the lead, barking at them.

"What's going on here?" He made sure to have an authoritarian tone to his voice.

"Please," one of the youths gasped. "You have to go and see."

"There's a body in there," another said.

Had he heard that right? A body? Surely they were having him on. "A body? What do you mean? You know you're trespassing, right?"

"We know, we'll go if you want. But you have to look, please."

"Yeah, right," Alan commented. "Pull the other one."

"Please, you have to believe us," another said, and Alan could see the sincerity in his eyes.

"We're not lying," the girl said, looking up through tear-stained eyes. "I'll go with you. I'll show you."

There was something about the way they were talking, the way they came across—it was so genuine, so honest. He didn't know what they'd seen, and wasn't convinced it was, in fact, a dead body, but maybe it was something in the darkness that looked similar to a body, or just a trick of the light.

"Where is it?" Alan asked as he gave Brutus the signal to calm down.

"In there."

"Inside," said another. "Go into the main room, and then into the side room on the left, it's there."

Alan narrowed his eyes. He knew the room well, and it wasn't that dark in there, either. He was also aware of what the procedure would be, on the tiny chance they were telling the truth. They would have to remain here to be questioned.

So he figured he'd make use of them.

"Show me," he asked.

"I'm not going back in there," one of the boys said, as the others got up and resigned themselves to the task at hand.

"You are, and if there is a body in there, you'll need to stay here so the police can talk to you."

"The police?"

"Fuck," one of them cursed.

"Show me the way," Alan pressed.

The girl was the first to move. The boys followed, and Alan brought up the rear. Making his way up through the loading dock, he followed the quartet through the bay, into the main room and the massive hunks of machinery that stood silent on the dirty factory floor.

They moved left but stopped short of reaching the door. As Alan caught up to them, the girl pointed. "It's in there.

Alan looked over at the open door and felt a sense of dread grow deep in the pit of his stomach that he'd not felt in a while. Brutus sniffed the air and then started to bark in the direction of the room.

"Stop, Brutus," Alan said, chastising the dog, but he wouldn't stop, which was bizarre. He never disobeyed a command like that. Alan frowned, his unease growing as he looked up at the doorway.

What dark secrets would the room hold?

Steeling himself with a long cleansing breath, he gritted his teeth and concentrated on placing one foot in front of the other. Were they having him on? Were these kids pranking him?

His mind raced with all kinds of possibilities regarding what was about to happen, and very few of them were good or pleasant.

Each step revealed more of the room as Brutus continued to pull and bark despite his best efforts to calm him.

As he was about level with the door, Alan felt his stomach flip and then drop as an old chair came into view, along with the slumped body that was sat in it. The stench in here was nauseating. He couldn't help but stare at the thing and the black pool of dried blood that covered the floor beneath the chair.

"Oh, shit…"

4

"So, this'll be your office," Kate said, opening the door to the side room and stepping inside. Jon followed and surveyed the modest space with its desk, chairs, filing cabinets, shelves, and an old leather sofa in one corner.

It was a nice space and more than adequate for his needs.

"Alright, thanks," he replied and moved around the desk to sit in his chair and test it out. It creaked as he settled his weight into it, but was otherwise perfectly comfortable.

"Happy?"

"Ecstatic," Jon replied, deadpan.

Kate leant against the door frame and regarded him, tilting her head sideways. "So, what brings a northerner like you, all the way down here then?"

"Well, it's not the prices of things, that's for sure."

"Heh, yeah. Things can be a little more expensive around here."

"You're not kidding. I was looking at house prices and nearly had a heart attack."

"You'll do alright on a DCI's salary."

"You think? I reckon I'll be living on pot noodle for the foreseeable."

"So why'd you come?"

"Damon invited me," he replied, opening the drawers in the side of the desk, finding them empty for the most part.

"Damon? And you just said yes?"

"We go back a ways," Jon replied. "He used to be a DI in my unit."

"Oh, really? That's interesting. I had no idea."

"Sir?"

Jon looked up to see Nathan step into the doorway beside Kate. "What's up, Halliwell?"

"I'll be out most of the day. I'll be at Guildford Crown Court, watching a case we handed to them."

"Which one?"

"Abban Devlin."

Jon noticed Kate close her eyes and sigh at the name. Nathan glanced at her and put his hand on her shoulder. She smiled briefly but looked troubled.

"I saw that on the news," Jon remarked, remembering the news report this morning in the hotel room.

"Yeah," Nathan replied. "His wife's kicking up a stink. Looks like she's trying to single-handedly reignite the Troubles."

"So that was your case, this Abban guy? You arrested him?"

"Yeah," Nathan replied. "The last one before we became the SIU. It looks like he's going to go down for kidnapping and a few other bits. The Irish government wants him extradited to stand trial for murder over there, too."

"Impressive. I hope I can live up to these high standards."

"I'm sure you will," Kate replied.

"I'll catch you later," Nathan said and patted Kate's shoulder. She touched his hand in return.

"See ya, Fox."

"Laters, Irish."

Jon watched him go and fixed Kate with a questioning look. "I thought I detected a hint of an Irish accent in you."

"It's from my family on my mother's side. She was Irish and I spent a lot of time there growing up."

"I see. And Fox?"

Kate smiled. "I'll let Nathan explain that one, or maybe you can figure it out for yourself," she replied with a wink, before retreating from the doorway.

Jon nodded, and smiled to himself, stifling a smirk. He shook his head, turning it away from Kate as she walked away. What had gotten into him, today? He'd only been away from Nottingham for a couple of days, and he was already eyeing up one of the detectives on his team.

He needed to get his head into the game, and looked around the room once more.

The office wasn't huge, but it would certainly be enough for his needs. He fired up his PC and was surprised to see a modern operating system powering it, rather than an ancient crumbling edition of Windows 95 or something. They really did have all the mod cons.

The computer got to a login screen, and Jon grimaced. He needed to get himself registered on the system.

Getting up from his desk, he was already having ideas about what he wanted to bring in and have to hand. He'd need to visit his storage locker, where he'd dumped all his stuff after moving down.

Looking out over the desks and the people sat at them, he noticed there were several empty ones. The core team sat closest to his office and the main doors, and beyond them were several civilian investigators that helped handle much of the drudgery of office work and trawling through databases and such.

"Can someone get me my login details for the system?" he called out.

"I'll get them, sir," DC Dion Dyer replied.

"Thanks, son."

"Sir?" DS Rachel Arthur called out. "I've just had a call, looks like we've had a case come in."

"Excellent, and on day one, what are the chances?"

"I'll print off the details."

"Thanks, I'll take this on. Kate?"

"Sir?"

"You're with me."

"Sir," she replied and stood up, pulling her coat on as Rachel finished printing the details off and handing them to her.

"We'll take my car," Jon suggested, waving his keys at her.

"Be still my beating heart," she quipped. "Come on, let's go."

They headed downstairs, Kate opening the doors as they went with her ID badge.

"Thank you," he said as they passed through another door.

"That's all you needed me for, isn't it?"

"I was hoping you wouldn't notice," Jon replied as they walked through reception.

"Sir?" the woman on the desk called out.

"Yello."

"I've got your new ID badge, here you go."

He took the badge with his photo and details on it and slung it around his neck. "Thanks."

Heading outside, Jon led Kate over to the car and proceeded to press his key fob fifteen times before it finally unlocked. I'll need to put a new battery in it before long, he thought, as they climbed into the vehicle.

"So, where are we headed?"

"The edge of Epsom," Kate replied. "Turn right, I'll direct you."

"Gotcha," he replied and manoeuvred out of the car park

"This reminds me of my first day on the Murder Team," Kate commented, a wistful tone to her voice.

"Oh?" Jon replied.

"Yeah. First day here, in this building, I was out on a case within moments of stepping into the place."

"And how did that turn out?"

"Alright, in the end. I was partnered with Nathan by the previous DCI and sent into the deep end on a pretty messed up case."

"How messed up?"

"A local businessman had been tied to a tree and sacrificed," she replied. Jon glanced over.

"Sacrificed? Really?"

"Oh yeah. It's not all tea and cakes with the vicar around here, you know. We have our fair share of crazies too."

"Doesn't everywhere?"

"Ain't that the truth."

"So, how did it turn out," Jon asked. "This sacrifice case of yours?"

"We found him. He was just a local family man, with a wife and kid who had no idea what he was up to. It was pretty messed up. He's in prison now."

"It's mad, isn't it? I've seen that kind of thing too. They seem like normal people. Just like, nice, you know? But they lead this double life of slaughtering people when they're away from the family home. It's madness, really."

"Yeah. This guy, though, he was part of something bigger… well… let's not get into that now. But yeah, that was one hell of an introduction into being a detective."

"And yet, you survived to tell the tale."

"The scars might not be visible, but they're there, trust me," Kate remarked, again she sounded introspective. Jon could tell her first case had left an impression on her and would be something she carried with her for a while. He could understand that though. The first few cases of many a detective were often the ones that shaped your worldview, especially if they were as shocking as Kate's sounded.

Jon nodded. "I believe it. I think we all carry some kind of scars, especially once you've been in this job long enough. They might not always be obvious, but they're there. Broken marriages, estranged kids, depression, PTSD, I've seen it all."

"I think it takes a certain type of person to do this job," Kate said.

"Oh, for sure."

"So, you married or anything?" she asked. "Did you bring your family down with you?"

Jon smiled and smirked. "No. I'm single. Nothing to keep me away from the office but myself." He wondered about asking her the same question but wasn't sure it was appropriate.

"I can relate," Kate replied, and Jon quickly reversed his decision, taking her comment as permission.

"You're single too?"

"Yeah, for now. So's Nathan. What a sad old bunch of loners."

"Don't knock it. It's us loners that keep these people safe," he commented, waving towards the other passing cars.

"I suppose," she replied and gazed out the window.

Jon concentrated on the road ahead and they sat in silence for a while, until he realised he'd need to make a choice on which roads to take. They were nearing Epsom, but he felt sure Kate had mentioned it was on the outskirts.

"Which way?" he asked. She didn't answer. Looking over, she was still gazing out the window. "Hey, Kate?"

"Huh?"

"Hi, welcome to the land of the living, I'm Jon."

"What? Oh, shit. Sorry. I'm away with the fairies."

"I thought you seemed a little distracted."

"Yeah, I'm fine. Just a lot on my mind."

"Like what?" Jon pressed.

"Oh, don't worry about it. Turn right here."

"Okay," he replied, letting it drop.

It didn't take them long to navigate to the crime scene, and Jon was soon pulling up alongside other vehicles, marked and unmarked on the side of the road before they got out and passed through the Police line without issue, the officer on duty signing them in as they passed.

"Aaah, well, well, well. O'Connell, I see you have some fresh meat for the grinder."

"Dyson," Kate replied to the PC was he walked over.

"So, where's Fox, then?"

"Guildford Court House, one of ours is in the dock," she replied. "This is DCI Pilgrim."

The PC, a tall thin man, turned to him and smiled. "Sir," he said. "I take it you're the new team leader then?"

"Aye," he replied. "That's about the long and short of it."

Dyson narrowed his eyes at him. "Judging from that accent, you're not from around here, then?"

Jon shook his head. "Nope. I'm from Nottingham."

"A northerner?" he replied with a raised eyebrow. "No offence, sir."

"None taken," he replied. "So, what've you got for us then?"

"Well, it's not quite as strange as the ones you've had recently," he said to Kate.

"Good," she replied.

They started down the track with its cracked concrete and overgrown trees and bushes on either side, and they soon passed a porta-cabin on their left. Jon craned his neck to look inside, only to be met by the face of a large dog that jumped up to look out the window. It barked as they passed, making Jon jump.

"Security station," Dyson said. "The body was reported by the guard who was on duty. There were some kids here who found it and triggered the passive infrared sensors in the building. They took him to the body, and then he called it in."

"And where are they now?" Jon asked.

"We have them. They're here, onsite."

"Good, we'll need to take statements from them."

"Of course," Dyson replied, and led them through the open gates, past other officers and police vehicles until the road opened up into a wide-open space, surrounded by wild, overgrown trees and undergrowth. In the centre of the cracked concrete area, Jon regarded the derelict buildings and the desolate atmosphere they gave off.

"Well, this is cheery," Jon remarked and looked over at Kate with a wry smile, but she wasn't looking at him. She eyed the building cautiously with a troubled expression. "Everything okay?" he asked.

"Yeah, fine," she replied as they walked down the side of the building and around to a loading dock. Outside, the

SOCOs had set themselves up. Vans had been parked up and white tents had been erected between them where people busied themselves. Many of them wore white coveralls with gloves, masks, and goggles.

"Kate," one of the figures in white said walking over. "Good to see you."

"Sheridan," Kate replied. "This is Jon Pilgrim, the new DCI with the SIU. Jon, this is Sheridan Lane."

"Nice to meet you, sir," Sheridan said. "I work in the same building and lead the SIU's SOCO team."

"A pleasure," Jon replied and offered his hand. He couldn't make much out about her as only her eyes were visible, but it looked like she was smiling beneath her mask.

Sheridan raised her hands and wiggled her fingers rather than take his offered hand. "Sorry, no can do."

"Oh, of course."

"Get suited up, I'll take you in. Jo, Stel, can you get these two some gear?"

Within moments they'd pulled on the protective clothing. Jon fiddled with the hood and mask until he felt relatively comfortable in it and then followed Sheridan into the building through the loading dock. They walked through the main factory floor and up to a side room.

Sheridan walked in and stood to one side, allowing Jon to look the scene over.

"Where are we in the process?" he asked.

"The divisional surgeon's been and gone and pronounced life extinct," she replied.

"Excellent, always good to know she's dead," he replied as he looked at the body. It sat slumped in the chair, leaning forward, her head lowered, her dark copper hair falling around her face. Her body was held in place by whatever was keeping her hands bound behind the chair. There was an awful lot of blood on the floor beneath her, mainly towards the back. "Wouldn't want that being challenged in court."

Sheridan nodded. "The Photographer has also made his pass, so we have stills and video of the scene. Now it's our turn."

"First impressions?" Jon asked. Being careful where he stood, he walked into the room. The girl was still dressed, wearing jeans and a top, and he noticed there was a phone and a purse on the floor, a short distance away from the body.

"From what I can see, it looks to me like she was tortured before she was killed."

"Really?" Kate asked.

"Come round here," Sheridan directed them.

Jon did as she asked and moved to the back of the room, behind the body. Sheridan crouched down beside the chair, and without touching, directed his attention to the victim's hands.

"She's been cuffed to the chair, and there's evidence of bruising around her wrists, suggesting she'd been struggling against them."

"She's missing two fingers," Jon said as he crouched down and took a closer look at the victim's right hand, which was missing its pinkie and ring fingers. The severed digits were still on the floor beneath the chair.

"Done before she was killed. In fact, I believe they played a part in her death. A small part, mind."

"She bled out?" Jon replied, frowning at the long cuts up the inside of both her arms. They were deep, and her hands were covered in the dried blood that had pooled beneath her.

"That seems to be the case," Sheridan answered. I've spotted some bruising on her face too. So I think she was punched, at least twice, then had her fingers cut off before he finally slashed her wrists and let her bleed to death."

"He?" Jon asked.

Sheridan shrugged. "Just hedging my bets. We have some footprints which we think point to a person who part-carried, part-dragged her in here. Given the weight of an unconscious body, I'd say it was most likely a man."

"Probably," Jon admitted. Most killers were male. He stood and took a wider view of the scene. "Okay, he brought her to a derelict building, cut two of her fingers off, and then let her bleed to death. This was deliberate and calculated."

"He's trying to tell us something," Kate agreed.

"Exactly. So first off, why here? Why a derelict building?"

"It's quiet and well away from the public," Kate replied.

"It is," Jon agreed. "So maybe this was just a practical choice."

Kate nodded.

"But there's security here," Jon said, challenging her. "So, maybe it isn't quite so straight forward. Maybe the choice of this location has a deeper meaning."

"Like what?"

"I've no idea. We need to do some research, look at the history of the building maybe, where it is on a map, that kind of thing."

Kate shrugged. "Ok, so what about the fingers?"

"I don't know," Jon replied. "But that's clearly some kind of statement. There's meaning to that action. I think there's meaning to the cuffs too, and I think that might give us our first clue."

"Cuffs could suggest the police," Kate replied.

Jon nodded. "But in what capacity? Does he blame the police for something? Or maybe he wants us to see something?"

"He could just be drawing our attention to her hand."

"Yeah, maybe. Or is it to do with his past? Is he telling us who he is? I think we need to look into these cuffs and see if we can track them down, where he bought them, and see if we can track him that way."

"We should also look through the database of former police officers, see if something jumps out at us."

"Good," Jon replied, as Kate's phone rang in her pocket. She looked surprised and stepped out of the room to answer it.

Jon watched her go as he heard her greet Nathan. Returning his attention to the room, his eyes came to rest on the purse and phone. "So, who is she?" He looked up at Sheridan.

"According to the purse and the ID that's inside it, she's Harper Richards. We'll take her prints and DNA and get that confirmed."

"Thanks."

"We've got photos of the ID, and the other secondary identifiers, I'll get that sent over to you, too."

"Great."

"How's she been?" Sheridan asked.

"Who, Kate? She's alright. A bit distracted maybe."

"Figures."

"Why?" Jon asked.

"It'll be the case that Nathan's at today. She arrested him."

"So, it's personal."

"Something like that," Sheridan replied. She seemed cagy about it too, and it didn't look like she wanted to talk about it, so he didn't press the matter.

"Fair enough."

Moments later, Kate returned to the room. "Sorry about that."

"Everything alright? Do you need to do anything or…"

"No," Kate cut in. "I want to work."

"Alright," he replied and decided he'd keep a close eye on her. She seemed troubled by something, and he didn't want her making any bad decisions due to whatever was on her mind. "Let's go and talk to the security guard and find out his story."

5

Walking back into his office, Jon dumped his coat and walked back out to where Kate, Rachel, Dion, and Faith were working. Kate hadn't even sat down and was already clicking away on her PC.

"Alright, so what's come in so far?" Jon asked.

Talking to the security guard and the teenagers who'd found the body had taken a while, but they hadn't known much. The kids were just exploring what they had thought was a cool building. Alan, the guard, had been a little more useful. He knew that whoever had come in and dumped the body hadn't triggered any of the PIR sensors in the building.

But the sensor's coverage wasn't complete, he'd admitted, and they were fairly obvious to anyone who knew what to look for, making them easy to avoid. The killer either actively avoided them, or he'd just gotten lucky in choosing his entry and exit points.

All of which was interesting information, but it didn't really help them. Clearly, it had been too much to expect there to be video surveillance on the site. But then, he guessed that the value of the site was the land and not really the building. So all they had to do was to stop idiot kids from going in there, falling through a rotting floor, and killing themselves.

"We've got copies of the victim's ID," Kate said.

"Run it," Jon suggested. "Let's see if she's got a record."

"I'll see what I can dig up about her," Dion offered.

"Great, thanks," Jon replied as Kate entered her name into the system. Within moments, a bunch of details appeared, and it was clear that Miss Harper Richards had a record."

"Oh, yeah, she's known to us," Kate announced. "She's got a record for drug possession, several counts. I have an address here too. Looks like her mother's."

"Anyone linked to her case?" Jon asked, curious to see what connections she had.

"Um, hold on…" Kate replied, drawing her words out as she read the screen. There's a couple of names, her friend Victoria Spencer, and the guy she was getting the drugs from, Seth Bailey."

"A local dealer?"

"Yeah, he's got a much longer record, but he's not been picked up for anything for a few months. Also, the date of her offence was a while ago. Last year."

"Okay."

"Hmm, well, it also looks like her mother called the police, um, this morning and reported her missing."

"Aaah, well that lines up with what we know so far," Jon remarked. "Anything else?"

"Only that the photo we have on record for her is a good match for the one on her ID, it's certainly the same girl."

"I want to speak with the mother. Is there a father on the scene?"

"I have his name here, but it says he and her mother are separated," Kate replied.

"Broken family, got it. Okay, Kate, you and I should head to the mother's place. We need to get her to ID the photo, and then we'll talk to her, see if she knows anything. In the meantime, Rachel, I want you to get some officers to help you, and go door to door around her mother's house. Let's see if anyone spotted anything unusual.

"Will do," Rachel replied, and got to work.

"I'll come with you to the mother's," Faith suggested.

"I was about to say the same thing," Jon replied.

"I'll take my own car. I'll probably be there longer than you will."

"Agreed. Kate, let's go," Jon said, grabbing his coat. She nodded and followed him out.

As Jon drove through the Surrey countryside, Kate sat quietly in the passenger seat, looking out through the side window, watching the world go by. Something was clearly bothering her and seemed to have her daydreaming the day away.

He wondered if this would become a problem and jeopardise the case. If the situation that was apparently playing out at the Guildford courthouse was on her mind, maybe she should be there and not Nathan.

But if she didn't want to do that, then the integrity of this current investigation needed to be taken into consideration.

He liked Kate, from the short time he'd spent with her, and wanted to give her the benefit of the doubt, but this was the police, not a high street shop. Integrity, diligence, and professionalism were paramount. They had to be beyond reproach in all things. He'd give her a chance, and would need to have a chat with her if he thought it was jeopardising the case, but so far, he didn't think it was.

Looking over at her again, he decided to probe a little deeper.

"You got a call from Nathan earlier," he began, and Kate turned to look at him. "Is everything alright?"

"Yeah, I think so. The case seems to be going well. I think we got our man."

"That's good then, right?"

She nodded. "Yeah, it is."

"You still look worried, though."

"Sorry. Don't worry about me, I won't let it affect my work," she replied. "It was a big case and I want to see justice served."

Jon nodded but felt there was more to it than that. She seemed to have a personal stake in it for whatever reason.

"Okay, good. I just wanted to be sure," he replied, hesitant to push it further.

"I know. Sorry."

"Stop saying sorry," he replied with a smile.

"Sorry. I'll stop saying sorry. Apologies," she replied, a grin spreading over her face.

"Oh, it's like that, is it?"

"Sorry?"

"Piss off."

"Sorry."

"Ugh."

Kate laughed—a most welcome sound.

6

Pulling up at a house in the suburbs of Epsom, Jon looked over at Kate who was checking something on her phone. In the rearview mirror, he watched Faith pull up a short distance behind them and get out.

"Anything new?" Jon asked.

"Yeah," Kate replied. "Sheridan posted an update, looks like the body's fingerprints match the ones for Harper that we have on the database."

"So, there's no doubt now that we have the right girl, then."

"Looks that way," Kate replied with a sigh and stuffed her phone in her jacket pocket. She looked past him towards the house they were parked outside of. She looked sad, and Jon knew exactly what she was feeling. This was a part of the job that he hated the most. Delivering the news of someone's death was always a heart-wrenching moment. Some took it better than others, but when it was someone's child like this was, you could almost see them shatter right before your eyes.

"I hate this bit," Kate said.

"I know," Jon agreed. "Let's get it done, though."

Kate nodded. Jon climbed out of the car as Faith walked over to join them.

"Ready?" he asked her. She nodded.

"Her name's Iris Richards," Kate said as they started up the driveway of the semi-detached council house. The road was quite nice, as far as Jon was concerned, even if this was council housing. Cars lined the street and were parked up in the driveways of the boxy dwellings. It was easy to spot those who were making the most of things and keeping their properties in good shape, while others had been left to fall to wrack and ruin.

Iris's house lay somewhere towards the middle of that range. The grass could do with a cut, the brushes needed a trim, and there were a few too many weeds poking through the paving slabs, but the house wasn't in bad condition. Two cars were parked up on the driveway, both of them were small, economical hatchbacks designed for city living. Jon raised an eyebrow at them and wondered if one of them belonged to Harper.

Knocking on the door, they didn't need to wait long before the door opened, and a middle-aged woman appeared. Jon spotted an immediate likeness between the photos of Harper he'd seen, and the woman before him, which only cemented the certainty that they were speaking to the right person.

"Hello?" Iris said.

"Good morning. I'm DCI Jon Pilgrim with the Surrey Police." He held up his warrant card. "Are you Iris Richards?" Jon asked.

"I am," she replied, and Jon could see the slowly growing look of horror on her face. "Is this about Harper?"

"May we come in?" Jon asked. "We'd like to talk to you."

"Is this about Harper?" she asked again, her tone insistent.

"I'd really rather talk inside," Jon pressed, not keen on doing this on the doorstep.

"Is it? Tell me, please. I just need to know."

"Yes," Jon replied, simply.

"She's dead, isn't she?"

Jon went to say yes but found the word caught in his throat. Instead, he nodded. "I'm sorry."

Jon watched the cracks appear. Her breath caught, the strength in her legs seemed to fade, and she collapsed to the floor as a body racking sob came from deep inside her. Faith stepped past as Jon reached to help. Faith was down beside her in a moment, and between the three of them, they helped her inside, closing the door behind them.

In the end, Jon left Faith to it. They'd all been trained in dealing with this kind of thing, but Faith had way more training and experience. So they left her to it. He ended up sitting in the kitchen, reviewing the case on his phone, while Kate moved back and forth between the sitting room and other parts of the house, running errands, getting tissues, and making drinks.

Jon watched Kate work, helping out where he could, and saw a woman dedicated to her job, who'd put aside her worries and concerns to do what needed to be done.

He found his confidence in her grow as the minutes ticked by. While she might be worried about the court case, she wasn't letting it interfere with her work here.

She was a strong, capable woman. She kind of reminded him of Charlotte in that way. She'd also been a powerful force in his life and had put up with the rigours of his job with aplomb. It was a trait that he found endlessly attractive, and he saw it in Kate as well.

"…and I've got Dion hunting through CCTV from the roads around the factory. Just on the off-chance we find something," Jon commented.

"Such as a man carrying a body through the streets?" Kate quipped.

"Don't joke, I've heard of more brazen acts than that."

"I don't doubt it," Kate replied as she finished adding milk to another round of drinks.

"She's ready to answer some questions," Faith said, poking her head out of the front room.

"Great," Jon replied and walked with Kate, who carried a tray with another round of teas on it, into the room.

Iris sat on the sofa holding a tissue and sniffing, her eyes were red and bloodshot from the emotional trauma she was going through, and she looked up at him with almost pleading eyes.

He'd seen the same look in the relatives of other victims and nodded to her. "How are you feeling?"

"I'm... I'll survive, I guess."

"That's good enough," Jon replied.

"Tell me what happened to her," Iris asked. "Faith says she was murdered? Is that right?"

"That's right. I'm sorry for your loss, Mrs Richards. I truly am, but we need to ask you a few questions. Is that okay?"

"Of course. Anything I can do to help. But please, what happened to her?"

"We're still trying to work that out. We found her in an abandoned factory."

"A factory? Oh, God," she gasped. "Oh, my poor baby," Iris muttered as she sobbed again.

Jon waited, and let Iris ride out the emotions until she'd calmed down.

"What do you want to know?"

"Anything you can tell us, basically. So, it looks like, from our records, that Harper lived here, with you?"

"No, she lived with her boyfriend, Seth. Seth Bailey."

Jon raised an eyebrow, remembering the name from Harper's criminal record. Was she dating the young man who'd been dealing her drugs? "For how long now?"

"A few months. She moved out. She still visited, though."

"So, she wasn't here the night of her death?"

"No, she was. She came home yesterday after arguing with Seth. Sounded like it was a bad one, so she came here to get away."

Jon wasn't one to jump to conclusions, but he made note that they'd need to look into Seth Bailey. "Alright, Mrs Richards, can you go through what happened yesterday, and anything else you can think of?"

She sighed, taking a deep breath to steady herself. "I never liked Seth. She started dating him nearly a year ago, I think. I don't know how they first met, she was always a bit vague on that. She said he was just a part of the group of friends she hung out with. But he always had a way about him. He was brash and just way too self-confident, you know?"

"I understand," Jon replied. "Please, go on."

"Anyway, Harper wasn't the same after her dad left. It strained our relationship, and we couldn't seem to get along like we used to."

"Her father, that's Peter Richards, right?" Jon asked, checking his notes.

"That's right. Neither of us has seen him in years. I've got no idea where he is now."

"And Harper never saw him?"

"Not that I know of. It hit her pretty hard, and that's when she started getting into trouble. She was never quite the same after that."

"We're going to have to track him down," Jon replied.

Iris nodded. "I understand."

"So, yesterday?"

"She just turned up on my doorstep last night. I knew she'd been crying, but she didn't seem to want to talk about it at first. I kept asking, and she eventually told me she'd fought with Seth, but she wouldn't tell me why or what it was about. I think I annoyed her because she stormed out and went for a walk." Iris paused as fresh tears welled up in her eyes. "She never came back."

"She didn't take her car?"

"No. That's not unusual though. She's always liked walks. She often went on them to clear her head when she lived here."

"Do you know where she went?"

Iris shook her head. "I tried calling her and texting her, but she never answered."

"Is that unusual?"

"No," she replied with another sigh. "Not especially. She was always such a wilful girl. Wouldn't listen to anyone, always knew her own mind. She'd often go days without contacting me, even if I'd been texting. But I knew something wasn't right. I just knew it…" Her voice cracked again and she stifled a sob.

"I'm sorry, Mrs Richards. We'll do our best to help you. Did she say anything else? About Seth?"

"She said they had a fight, an argument. He got really angry at her over something. I don't know what, but she was… She looked scared."

"I see," Jon replied, mentally assigning another strike to Seth.

"He did it, didn't he? Seth. He killed her."

"I wouldn't like to say, Mrs Richards. It could be anyone at this point."

"I knew he was trouble. I always said it. I told her. But she wouldn't listen."

"Do you know where Seth lives?"

Iris shook her head. "No, sorry. Harper was always cagy about it. I don't think she wanted me to see it, or know where she was. Her little way of telling me she didn't need my help. All her post still comes here, too."

"Okay. I'm sure we'll be able to figure it out.."

"Good. You know, I'm sure he did it. The more I think about it, the more it makes sense. I don't know what they were fighting over, but that has to be it. It must be him."

Jon had to admit, it did sound compelling. But the way Harper was killed, it didn't say crime of passion. It said just the opposite.

Beside him, Kate's phone rang. Apologising, she got up and rushed out of the room to take it. Jon watched her go and wondered if that would be Nathan again.

"Okay, thank you, Mrs Richards. I think we have everything we need for now. Faith will stay with you, take a more detailed statement, and help with anything you need. But we'll leave you for now. You've been really helpful. Thank you."

"Of course. Anything I can do, please just let me know."

"We will, thanks," he said and got up. Faith followed him out into the hall where Kate finished her call. "Nathan?"

Kate nodded. "All done?"

"For now," Jon replied before he turned to Faith. "Are you alright here?"

"I'll be fine. I'll stay for a while and make sure she's okay, and see about arranging someone to come over and stay with her. I'll take that statement too."

"Thanks, Faith."

She nodded and returned to the front room.

"Shall we go?" Jon asked.

"Yeah. We need to make a slight detour on the way back to the station, though."

7

"So, any updates from Nathan?" Jon asked.

"Not much, no," Kate replied. "I think there are a few more days left in the court case yet."

Jon nodded. "So, this guy, Abban. What did he do?"

"Kidnapped an old lady, amongst other stuff," Kate replied. "He's a piece of work."

"Sounds like it." Jon had a distinct feeling there was more to it than that, but again, he didn't really feel like pushing things too much. There was something about the Devlin case that had its claws in Kate, but she just kept dodging his questions and being vague. He could pull rank and find out more, but he didn't want to do that. He'd much rather wait for her to open up to him in her own time.

Besides, they had an active case going on and couldn't afford to get too distracted.

"So, the Seth angle seems like it might turn something up for us," Kate commented.

"He's high on the list of suspects," Jon agreed. "This whole thing stinks."

"Drug dealer turned boyfriend. Yeah, like that's not a recipe for disaster. I don't know what gets into people sometimes."

"Maybe she liked the rough ones?"

Kate smirked. "Yeah, maybe. Looks like it backfired on her though. Iris wasn't big on details. Do you think their fight turned violent?"

"I wouldn't be the slightest bit surprised," Jon replied.

"Yeah, me neither. Whatever it was, it was serious enough for Harper to run to her mother, even though their relationship doesn't sound great."

"Well, we have her phone," Jon said. "Maybe that will shed some light on Harper's relationship with Seth, her mother, and maybe even her father."

"You never know," Kate agreed as Jon navigated his way into Guildford. Kate gave him directions until he drove down a side road and passed the city's cinema complex and came out in front of the courthouse. Jon spotted journalists and photographers out front on the steps, waiting for the next juicy morsel to drop into their lap.

"Oh look, it's the press. Great," Jon remarked sarcastically as he drove by the court's main entrance.

"Yeah," Kate agreed, sounding equally wary of them. "Drive round there, you can park in here," Kate suggested, indicating the car park that was opposite the building. Jon soon found a space and eyed it critically. "Jesus, *how* small is that space?"

"I'll get out now." Kate undid her belt.

"Sure," Jon replied, and once she'd exited the car, he spent the next few minutes cursing up a storm as he manoeuvred his Astra into the frankly tiny space. He could see other spaces nearby, and they looked just as tiny, if not more so.

Was this car park designed for Hot Wheels cars or something?

He eventually got it parked, and squeezed out the door, doing his best not to chip the paint on the car beside his.

"Well done," Kate said and gave him a mocking round of applause.

"You can drive the next time we come here," he replied.

"With pleasure," she answered and then pointed to her right. "I'll park in there, though."

Jon looked over at the enormous, spacious, multi-story car park next door to this obstacle course, and screwed his face up. "You could have said something."

Kate shrugged. "And ruin your fun?"

"Any scratches on this puppy, and I'll bill you for their repairs," Jon said, grumbling to himself.

"Why bother? They'll just blend in with all the other chips and scratches and add to the car's character."

"Its character?"

"Don't all surly DCI's need to drive a banged-up motor? It's part of the job description, isn't it?"

"I'm not surly," Jon protested. "I'm a fluffy teddy bear."

Kate laughed. "If you say so. I'll reserve judgement. I've only known you for a few hours."

"I'll be sure to be on my best behaviour then. Wouldn't want to get a bad report from Miss O'Connell."

"You do that. Otherwise, I'll be forced to get the cane out," Kate replied as they exited the car park and approached the courthouse entrance.

"Is that a promise?"

"You'll have to wait and see, teddy."

Jon laughed.

The waiting press ignored them for the most part and seemed to be focusing their attention on the main entrance. But as they approached the front doors, walking up the front steps, a blonde-haired man stepped up to them.

"DC O'Connell," the man called out.

"Oh shit," she whispered, just loud enough for Jon to hear. Kate turned and looked at the man. "It's *DS* O'Connell now, Chester. You know that."

"Of course, my apologies," he replied with a fake sincerity and smile that Jon could spot a mile off. "Care to comment on the case?"

"Not really," Kate replied as she continued to walk.

"Who's your new partner? Did you finally have enough of Nathan's theories?"

Kate ignored him, as they continued to approach the main front doors.

"Theories?" Jon asked.

"I'll tell you later," Kate replied with a smile as they walked into the building. Jon spotted Nathan right away, and they walked over to him.

"Hi," Nathan said in greeting. "Sorry to call you in. I got a lift here, but my ride back to the station got called away."

"It's okay," Kate replied. "How's it going?"

Nathan was about to answer but apparently noticed something as he suddenly moved past Kate. Jon turned and watched him step between her and an approaching woman.

"Oi, you! Kate. Come here, you bitch," the woman shouted. Jon recognised her right away as the woman he'd seen on TV this morning. Abban Devlin's wife, Faye.

"Hey, whoa, oh no you don't," Nathan said, standing in her way. Jon stepped forward too, putting himself between Kate and Mrs Devlin.

"You heartless fucking bitch. You set him up. You can't do this to him!" Faye shouted. "He's innocent!"

"Mum," a young man beside Faye called out, reaching out to pull her away. "Mum, please. She was just doing her job."

"Doing her... Piss off. You heard what she accused him of. He's no murderer. Come here, you cow!" she shouted again. "I'll show you!"

"Mum, stop, please. You'll get in trouble."

"I don't care."

"Mrs Devlin, that's enough," Nathan called out. "I know you're upset…"

"Upset?" she raged, trying to launch herself at Kate. Jon quickly stepped in the way and fended her off, only for her to scream at him and hold her hand up in a V-for-Victory sign. "Get out of my way, we'll win this."

By now, several other officers and guards had joined the fray. She was pulled away and moved off as she continued to proclaim Abban's innocence. Jon watched with fascination as Faye continued to rage and shout, calling Kate all the names under the sun.

He turned, to find her stood watching the scuffle with a troubled expression on her face. Nathan was still helping pull Faye away, having been caught up in the chaos.

"You okay?" Jon asked.

"Yeah, I'm fine. I don't think she likes me very much."

Jon laughed. "Yeah, no shit."

"We should get Nathan and go."

Jon nodded and looked over. Nathan slowly extracted himself from the knot of people and straightened his suit as he walked over.

"Well, that was a bit of excitement in an otherwise boring day."

Jon raised an eyebrow. "If you say so," he replied. Nathan probably didn't know about the case they were working on.

"Come on, let's get out of here," Kate urged.

"Good idea," Nathan agreed, and they started to walk out when a voice called out to them.

"Detectives?"

Jon looked around and spotted Faye's son, jogging over to catch them up. Jon moved to stand in his way. "What's up?"

The young man held his hands up in surrender. "Hey, I don't want any trouble," he said, looking past Jon to Kate. "I'm sorry for my mum. She just doesn't want to believe what my dad's been accused of."

"That's okay, Brendan," Kate replied.

"Thanks for coming over," Jon added, making sure there was an unsaid, 'piss off' in there somewhere.

"Okay. Sorry. I don't mean to take up your time. And, for the record, despite what my mum thinks, I believe you. My dad was always secretive. Now we know why."

"Okay, thanks," Kate replied.

"Bye," Jon said, moving between him and Kate.

The young man looked up, and after a beat, smiled. "Oh, okay. Yeah, bye," he said, and turned away, walking back towards where his mother was still making a scene.

The press had apparently gotten wind of the altercation and were already swarming around the entrance as they walked out. Several of them called out to Kate and Nathan, asking them questions or wanting a statement from them. It was chaos, and the shouted words mixed together, making it tough to make much out as Jon focused on keeping up with his colleagues and pushing through the scrum.

Luckily for them, it seemed that they were far more interested in the Devlins and the juicy story of Faye and her protests against the case, than they were in Jon's fellow officers.

They were soon through them and crossing the road, leaving the courthouse behind. Jon made a bee-line for the car, and a few moments later, they were on their way, leaving the city.

"So, how's the case going?" Kate asked Nathan from where she sat in the front passenger seat.

"If I had to guess, I'd say Abban will see some time inside. I can't see him getting off. Terry is still trying to take the heat for everything, though."

"Terry?" Jon asked.

Kate took a breath. "This was our last big case," Kate began. "It started with a robbery gone wrong. Terry Sims and his crew murdered an old man while they were trying to rob him. But from what we can tell, Abban was the one behind it all. Terry was just his thug."

"Oh," Jon replied. "And the kidnapping charges?"

"Abban and Co. were after an old, valuable book, but we got to it first and brought it to the station. Abban wanted that book, so he kidnapped my neighbour and tried to blackmail me into giving it to him."

"Wow," Jon replied, shocked at the details of the case. "No wonder you're invested." Kate nodded in reply, clearly affected by it. "Sorry you had to go through that."

"It's okay," she replied. "At least he'll see some time."

"He should," Nathan replied. "And then there's the murder he committed in Ireland. He's going to be extradited to Ireland in a few days to stand trial for that."

"Good," Kate replied.

"Sounds like you did your jobs," Jon commented. "You should be proud of yourselves."

"Heh," Kate chuckled, but it wasn't a terribly happy sound. "Yeah, I guess.

"So," Nathan began, "what have you guys been up to?"

Kate looked over at Jon with a single raised eyebrow. Jon returned the look, with an equally incredulous expression.

"Do you want to tell him, or should I?" Kate said.

"Tell me what?" Nathan asked.

8

"Right then," Jon said, sat at the head of the table in the dedicated incident room that they'd chosen to use for the case. A large free-standing whiteboard on casters stood to his right, displaying a photo of Harper when she was alive. Beside it, pictures from the crime scene picked out details such as the severed fingers, the cuffs, the cuts on her wrists, and the general location.

There was a family tree drawn up, as well as a list of known friends and associates. Seth was on there too, with a photo that Dion had pulled from police records.

Jon went over the case with them all. He described the crime scene and the timetable that the SOCO team and the Pathologist had worked out, plus the timing of the events that Iris Richards had provided.

"From what we can tell, it looks like Harper was snatched from the street close to where her mother lived. Given the approximate time of her death at around midnight, and the time she walked out of her mother's house at around 9 pm, that gives us a three-hour window. So we need to go through CCTV around her mother's place, and around the factory. My guess, based on what we know so far from the killing, is that this guy knows what he's doing. I would be surprised if we found something. But, you never know. Everyone makes mistakes sometimes, so let's get looking and keep our fingers crossed. Alright, Rachel, how's the door-to-door going?"

"We're still neck-deep in it, but nothing major to report yet. I think we have a couple of possible sightings of her shortly after she left her mother's which gives us an idea of her route, but that's all so far."

"Okay, good work, keep going. Dion, what about her phone? Anything there?"

"We've got the records of her calls and we have transcripts of her messages," he said and handed out copies of them. "There are a few things to note in there, which I've highlighted. There are some messages between Harper and Seth, with Seth apologising for the fight they got into. There's no mention of him hitting her, but it sounds like it got physical from what Harper says. On page three, you can see she says he hurt her and that she had a bruise."

"I see," Jon replied, reading the message.

"She's apologising to him here, too," Kate said, pointing to the page. Jon glanced at where Kate was pointing on her transcript and found it on his. Harper had written a suitably vague, 'Sorry for what I did,' note, but hadn't elaborated.

"Yeah," Dion replied. "Don't know what that's in regards to, though. Looks like she did something to annoy him, but it looks like she did it in retaliation for something he did."

"Looks like they had an acrimonious relationship," Jon remarked. There were huge gaps in the narrative of the messages, probably because they were doing much of their talking face to face, and using the messaging apps to supplement it when they were apart. What was clear, though, was that something had happened between them, something that was bad enough for her to go to her mother's house. But was it bad enough for him to murder her?

"What more do we know about Seth? Is he still dealing?" Jon asked.

"We've not picked him up for a while," Rachel replied. The last time was over six months ago, and that was for dealing again. But he's got previous for assault, possession with intent to supply, robbery, etc. etc. He's a career criminal."

"He was dating Harper when we last picked him up, then?" Jon asked.

"Yep. We have his current address too."

"Excellent, that will be our next port of call. Okay, her absent father. What do we have on him?"

"We're still looking into him, but it doesn't look like he lives locally anymore," Rachel replied.

"I saw some messages from him," Dion said, flicking through the transcript. "Yeah, here. Page six. Nothing earth-shattering, though."

Jon turned to the relevant page and scanned the messages. It was just Peter asking how her day was, what she was up to, and Harper messaging back.

"Okay, there's nothing in the messages. See what you can find out about him. Where is he these days? What's he doing? Who does he associate with? That kind of thing."

"Will do," Rachel replied.

"I don't think Iris knew Harper was in touch with her dad," Jon added.

"Maybe not," Kate agreed.

"Anything else?" Jon turned to Sheridan, who looked very different out of her crime scene gear with her long blonde hair tied up at the back of her head. "Anything about the crime scene?"

"No fingerprints, from what we can tell," Sheridan replied. "He was most likely gloved. The report from the pathologist came in. She found bruises on Harper's body, consistent with being strangled, and punched in the face. Several more elsewhere on her body that could suggest a fight or struggle. But there's no way to know if they were by the killer, or from the domestic with Seth. I've also entered the cuffs into the case's exhibits."

"Yeah, we got them," Dion replied. "We're looking into seeing if we can trace them."

Jon nodded his thanks to him.

"Other than that," Sheridan continued, "there's not much to go on."

"Okay, thanks, Sheridan. Right, Nathan, if you've finished with the Devlin case for the day, can you help Rachel with the door-to-door and the CCTV? Dion, keep digging. Kate, let's go and find Seth."

Kate nodded.

They were soon out on the roads again, making their way towards Sutton, and Seth's flat.

"Where's your heart taking you on this one, then?" Jon asked as he wound his way along the roads, between masses of leafy trees and views over the Surrey Downs.

"Mmm, well, the obvious choice is Seth. From their messages it sounds like Seth did something to piss Harper off, so she gave as good as she got, and annoyed him. That ended up in a fight, and we know the rest. So we know he was unhappy. But would that lead to him killing her in the way that we found her? I'm not at all convinced about that. Her killing was cold and calculating, and I think there's more to it than just a lover's tiff."

"Fair point, but to play devil's advocate, it's also clear that Seth is still involved in criminal activity, right? So how much do we really know about what kind of man he is? Couldn't he be another one of these double-life killers? A loving boyfriend at home, and a hardened criminal on the streets?"

"Sure, maybe. But I don't think it lines up right now. I think there's something we're still missing," Kate replied.

"I actually agree," Jon replied. "So, could that missing piece be her father?"

"An estranged, absent relative? Sounds compelling to me."

"Well, hopefully, Seth can answer some questions, and maybe we can rule him out."

"Wouldn't that be wonderful?" Kate replied with a smile.

Seth's home was one of countless flats in the Chaucer Gardens area of Sutton, towards the northern end of town. Jon pulled up outside one of the brown bricked, blocky, two-story affairs, and climbed out of the car, taking in the urban environment. Towering over the old, squat blocks that looked like they were well past their best, was a huge blue apartment block that was many stories high, and looked quite new.

"Do you think that's something for the people down here to aspire to?" he asked, pointing up at the blue tower.

"Lofty goals, and all that?"

"Something like that. So, where is it?"

"Up there," Kate replied, pointing to the block beside them

"Excellent, let's go," Jon replied and led Kate over the road. They walked in through a passageway and a door to a set of stairs that led up. Several teenagers sat on the steps and looked up at them with unimpressed expressions.

"Oi, oi. What do we have here then?" one of them commented.

"Check out the redhead," another added.

"Feisty," a third added.

"Afternoon, lads," Jon said in greeting, grimacing at their comments. "Any of you know Seth Bailey?"

"And what if we do?" one of them replied. "What's in it for us?"

"A sense of civic duty and accomplishment," Jon replied, his voice even.

"Yeah, piss off."

"Fair enough. Now, do you mind?" Jon replied, motioning that they wanted to get through.

"And what if we do mind?"

"Then I'll arrest you for obstruction," Jon replied, saying the first thing that came into his head. He couldn't be bothered messing about with these guys and wanted them out of his way.

"That's not a thing," one of them replied.

"You're a pig?" said another.

A third one snorted, making pig noises.

"It's pronounced, Po-lice-off-i-cer," Jon replied, sounding out the word in bits as if he was talking to a particularly dense individual. "Now come on, move it. Out of the way."

"Yeah, alright, don't get your knickers in a twist," the first boy answered as he stood and lead his friends past them and outside.

"I'd like to get in a twist with her knickers," another said, laughing as he bounced out of the passage. Jon looked back at Kate who rolled her eyes at him.

Nodding sympathetically, Jon led them up the steps to the balcony and around to Seth's flat. On reaching the door, Jon went to knock, only to find the door ajar. He frowned and glanced at Kate, who shared his expression. She took half a step back, as Jon reached into his coat and pulled out his baton.

He pushed the door open with the business end, and it squeaked as it swung in on his hinges. "Hello? Mr Bailey? It's the police."

As the door swung wide, Jon peered up the hallway and spotted a figure sat with his back against the wall.

Jon's breath caught in his throat for a moment. He thought he was looking at another dead body, but a second later, the head twisted, and the young man looked over at him. It wasn't Seth, but whoever he might be, he was bleeding from a cut on his head, sported a cracked lip, and held his torso with his arms.

"Help…me?"

"Crap," Jon cursed, and moved inside, checking his corners and making sure he wasn't about to be attacked, but the grotty rooms were empty of people. Instead, they looked like they could really do with a spring clean.

Satisfied no one was hiding in this first part of the flat, he joined Kate who was already crouched beside the young man.

"Hey, you alright?"

"What do you think?" the man muttered sarcastically.

"Yeah, stupid question. What hurts? Do you think you can move?"

"Everything bloody hurts."

"Can we get you to the sofa?" Kate replied.

The man sighed. "Yeah, thanks, that would be good."

Jon glanced at Kate, who smiled back. Between them, they helped him up and guided him to the threadbare seat. The man dropped into it, and visibly relaxed.

"That's better," he said with a sigh.

"I'll call an ambulance," Kate said and moved out of the room.

Jon watched her go and then turned to the young man. "What's your name?"

"Tom," he replied with a gasp and a wince. "Oof, I think they broke a rib."

Jon cringed, but he needed answers and he needed them now. "Tom, we're looking for Seth. Did he do this to you?"

"Seth? No! He wouldn't do this."

Good, Jon thought. "So, who did?"

"I don't know. A couple of guys, they were looking for Seth too."

"Oh?" More people were hunting for Seth? What was he mixed up in that would cause this to happen to his friend? "And you don't know who they were?"

"No idea. Sorry. You're the police, right?"

"Yeah, DCI Pilgrim."

"Pilgrim? Funny name."

Jon shrugged. "If you say so. Anyway, like I said, we're looking for Seth. Do you know where he might be? It's urgent."

"I'll tell you what I told them, I don't know. I've got no idea," Tom replied as Kate walked back into the room.

"Paramedics are on their way," she said.

Jon nodded. "This is Tom. He doesn't know who beat him up, but says they were after Seth," Jon replied, filling her in on what she'd missed, "and he doesn't know where Seth is."

Kate nodded and looked over at Seth quizzically. "You've got no idea? He didn't say where he was going?" Kate pressed.

"No," Tom replied. "He did tell me not to stay here, though."

Jon gave him a look. "He warned you?"

"Said it was dangerous. Wish I'd listened now."

I bet, Jon thought. "So, he knew someone was after him?"

"I guess," Tom replied. "Don't know why, though."

"Did it having anything to do with Harper?" Jon asked.

"No idea."

"Did you see the argument they had?"

Tom laughed and then doubled over in pain as he brought his humour under control. "Oh, shit. That hurt."

"Help's on its way," Kate reassured him.

"So, you did hear an argument?"

"Which one?"

Jon raised an eyebrow. By the sounds of things, they were either a naturally volatile couple, or things were not great between them. Still, he figured he'd best clarify his question. "Yesterday's argument."

"Yeah, I heard it. I don't get involved in their shit. Stayed in my room. They're always arguing, and then making up. Nothing new."

"Was there anything different about this one?"

"I don't know. I wasn't listening. Had my headphones on. When I came out, Harper was gone, and Seth was packing a bag. That's when he told me to get out of here."

Jon wondered about that. If that was when Seth got spooked, what had been the reason? Was it something Harper said, or was he planning something?

"Okay, so he might not have told you where he was going," Jon pressed, "but do you know anywhere he might go? Any friends of his or anything?"

Tom shrugged and then winced with pain. "No. I've met a couple of his mates, but I don't know where they live."

"Any names?"

"None that would help you."

"Try us," Kate suggested.

"Skeech and Ginger?" Tom replied.

Jon pulled a face and looked up at Kate, who rolled her eyes again.

"Right, wonderful. Thanks for that."

"I do have Seth's phone number though, would that help?"

Jon stared at Tom for a moment and blinked. "It might."

"Here, pass me my phone, it's on the table," Tom said and proceeded to hunt through his handset, wincing as he moved until he handed it to Jon.

Jon copied it down and replaced the phone on the coffee table. Moments later, the ambulance rolled into the estate, and the paramedics came and tended to Tom's wounds, before choosing to take him to St Helier's Hospital, not far from them.

Standing on the balcony outside the flat, they waited for the SOCO crew to turn up and take control of the scene.

"Another twist in the tale," Jon said.

"Looks that way," Kate replied. "So, Seth was in trouble with someone. Do you think this was related to Harper maybe?"

"It might have contributed to the fight if he was stressed over something."

"We need to find out who these guys are that attacked Tom."

Jon nodded as he looked out over the estate, and eyed a tall pole with a closed-circuit camera on top of it that was pointed in their direction. "I might have an idea about that."

9

"Try again," Jon suggested as he sat beside Kate at her desk.

"Sure," she answered, and dialled Seth's number once more. Jon could hear the phone ring on the other end of the line as Kate held the handset to her ear. But as before, the call went through to voicemail and Kate hung up.

They'd already left a message for him, urging him to get in touch with them as soon as possible. Jon had no idea if that would work, but it was worth a try, but by the same token, it wasn't worth leaving a bunch of messages either.

Running his hand through his mop-like hair, Jon sighed. "Alright, get that trace out on his mobile, let's see if we can triangulate it and get lucky. Keep trying to call him though."

"Will do." Kate nodded.

"So, let's think this through. They had an argument about something. We don't know what, but whatever it was, it was enough to make Seth want to leave the house and warn his flatmate to get out too."

"He must have found something out," Kate replied. "Something serious, by the looks of it. Not only did he warn Tom, but that warning was justified. Whoever came calling chose to use Tom to send Seth a message."

"Huh, yeah, you're right. Just like the person who killed Harper was sending a message."

"You think the way they killed Harper was a message for Seth?"

"I'd not thought about it that way round before, but it could be," Jon mused, wondering if they'd made the wrong assumptions. Whatever the case, one thing was clear, they didn't have enough information to go on, and things seemed to be getting more complicated by the minute.

"Okay, let's shelve that for now," John continued. "So, what would make Seth disappear like that?" Jon asked. "It must have been something he found out during the argument with Harper. Did she threaten him? Did she have friends?"

"Maybe he hit her, and then she called some mates in?" Kate suggested.

"Were those mates the ones who beat up Tom?" Jon turned that idea over in his head and thought about her departure to her mums. "Had she finally had enough of him and decided to try and end things? That might be why she went to her mother's, too."

Kate nodded. "It all fits. Harper ends things with Seth, he gets violent with her, so she runs home and calls some mates in. Her friends then beat up Tom, while Seth catches up with Harper and kills her."

"Yeah, but this is all speculation," Jon replied with a grumble. "We need proof, we need more information."

He thought they'd found Seth, back there at the flats. He'd hoped that things would begin to get wrapped up in a neat little package, but he should have known better. That never happened. Instead, the mystery deepened, and they were left with more questions than answers.

"Sir?" Dion called out.

"What's up?"

"I've put in the request for the security camera footage. Hopefully, it won't take too long to come through."

"Thanks," Jon replied with a nod to the DC. "Anything on Harper's dad?"

"I've been looking into that," Nathan cut in. "Rachel's got the door to door stuff handled, so I looked into Peter Richards."

"Fair enough. Did you find anything?"

"Not too much, but I found out he lives in Scotland now. I tried calling him, using the number from Harper's phone, but I've not had any luck so far."

"Alright, how about we get some local bobbies to pop over and knock on his door?"

"I was thinking the same thing, actually," Nathan replied. "I've already got the details of his local station."

"Excellent, Fox," Jon replied, using the nickname everyone else was using for him.

Nathan pulled a face. "Has Scully been talking to you?"

"Who's…?"

Nathan nodded to Kate, and suddenly Jon understood the dynamic of the names, although he didn't fully understand why. Was Nathan a conspiracy theorist? He didn't feel like he could ask him that, though, and chose to leave it for the time being.

Over the next few hours, Jon helped out where he could with the case, but ended up spending much of his time in his office, entering details into the case file as the evidence began to build.

Slowly, the afternoon turned into evening, and Jon was beginning to think about heading home for the night. As he closed one of the reports, Damon appeared and knocked on his door.

"Evening, Pilgrim," he said with a smile. "How's your first day been?"

"Hectic," he replied. "This new case has been leading us on a merry chase."

Damon nodded. "I've been keeping track. That first killing has all the hallmarks of a serial killer, but that doesn't really fit with your main suspect."

"No, it does not," Jon replied, with a sigh, sitting back in his chair. "I'd expect a more frenzied murder scene if it was a crime of passion."

"So, maybe you've not found your man yet."

"Maybe not, unless that's what he wants us to think."

"Round and round we go," Damon replied with a lopsided smile.

"Yeah. Reminds me of the good old days. You and me on the Nottingham CID?"

Damon nodded. "Those were good times. Seems like an age ago now though."

"Yeah, it does."

"So, what are you up to, tonight? Want to stop by the pub later?"

"Could do. I need to finish up a few things first, though."

"I'm not in a rush," Damon replied. "I can always find work to do."

"If you can't, I can find you something," Kate said as she walked up to his office door carrying two mugs. She smiled up at Damon. "We have more than enough work to go around."

Damon moved out of Kate's way, and she walked in, handing one of the mugs to Jon.

"Tea?" Kate asked.

"Oh, lovely. Thank you."

"I didn't know how you took it, so it's just got milk in it," she said.

"That'll do nicely. I take it as it comes. I've had all sorts over the years."

"Me too," she replied and turned to Damon as she sipped her drink. "Come to check up on him?"

"Just wanted to see how he was getting on," Damon answered. "But it looks like he has everything in hand. I'll see you later for that drink, okay?"

Jon nodded. "You can count on it."

"Good man," Damon replied and walked off.

"He's a different man, around you," Kate remarked once Damon was out of earshot. "He usually seems so uptight."

Jon nodded. "We have a history, so that's probably got something to do with it."

Kate nodded and sat on the sofa on the right-hand side of the room. "Aaah, what a day," she commented.

"Make yourself comfortable."

"I will," she replied, and stretched out, reminding Jon of a cat. He smirked to himself.

"Are you done for the day?"

"Just taking a break," she replied. "We're well past the end of our shift."

"Shifts? What are those?" Jon joked.

"Exactly," she answered, wagging her finger at him.

"So how do *you* think I did, today? How would you rank my performance?"

"Oh, certainly in my top ten of awesome police officers."

"Top ten? Not top five, or top three?"

Kate held her hand out and see-sawed it as she pressed her mouth into a thin line. "Meh, I think that's pushing it."

"Hah. Well, I'll reserve judgement on ranking you then."

Kate smirked. "Very wise."

"You do make a nice cuppa though, I'll grant you that. So you've got that going for you."

"Well, I'm thrilled. Does that mean I'm not bottom of the barrel?"

"You're just above the scum."

She laughed again. "You know how to charm a lady."

"Hey, I know all the best pick-up lines."

"Well, keep them to yourself, Romeo," she answered, widening her eyes for a moment as she took another sip from her mug.

Sitting up straight, Jon stretched out an arm in a dramatic movement. "What light from yonder window breaks."

Kate smirked, spraying tea halfway across the room. "Oh, shit," Kate said with a laugh.

A beat later, Nathan appeared at the door and looked over at Kate with a bemused look. "What on earth's going on in here?"

"Just listening to Shakespeare here," she replied, waving at him.

"Ignore her," Jon said.

"I already do," Nathan replied.

"Shut it, you," Kate said, having finally recovered from her laughing fit.

"What's up?" Jon asked him.

"The bobbies up in Scotland just got back in touch. They've been round to Peter Richard's place, but there's no one home, and there's a few days' worth of mail on the mat inside the house."

"Hmmm, interesting. I wonder where *he* is then?"

10

Stepping out of the halls of residence, Mollie pulled her gloves out of a pocket and slipped them on. Once they were in place, she stuffed her hands in her pockets, and strode across the courtyard between buildings, making for the edge of campus.

She knew where to go, and had done it before, but this was only her second time making the trip alone. She usually did it with Brad or Rupa. But, Rupa was still busy with her latest assignment, so she didn't have time. Brad though, he was just being lazy and making a point because he'd been over to buy the stuff more than anyone else.

He had a point, she supposed, and it was only fair that they shared the jobs.

That didn't mean she liked it, though.

Things were intrinsically different for a young woman heading out on her own as opposed to a guy, but despite that, she wanted to do her part. She'd had a few weeks off from these trips due to her uni work, so now it was time she pulled her weight.

Moving through the campus, Mollie was soon heading out beyond the grounds and into the city beyond. She took the usual route and made for the usual meeting spot.

She wondered what her parents would say if they knew what she was doing. They'd likely hate it and demand that she stop, but Mollie had no intention of doing that.

Getting high was fun!

And anyway, it was just a bit of African Black. It didn't really do you any harm. The rolling tobacco was worse. Besides, everyone was doing it. It was fun, that was all. Harmless fun.

Didn't they deserve a bit of fun after working so hard all day? Lord knows the tutors were working them to the bone this year. Things were getting serious, and she had to start thinking about what she was going to be doing once she left university. That time would soon come, and she'd need to be ready.

Walking up the street, Mollie took the next left into the second of the cut-throughs that would allow her to get to the destination she had in mind. Partway up, a street light lit the side road, and a white van was parked up just beside it.

As the evening had drawn in, a mist had started to form, making the glow from the street lamp bloom in the night air.

The van was new. She'd never seen it there before, but no one seemed to be around, so she didn't think much about it and just gave it a wide berth as she passed it.

That's when the shadows moved. Something strong grabbed her and pulled her into the darkness on the other side of the van. She tried to scream, but the attacker had their hand over her mouth. The van's side door was wide open, revealing only darkness and she was thrown into the back with her attacker on top of her. The door rolled shut behind him.

She struggled and kicked, fighting him off. She wanted to get free, to run back to her room and slam the door shut and never come out.

As she kicked and fought, she saw metal glint in the dim light coming in through the front window screen. A second later, a sharp, cold pain lanced up through her leg. She screamed, but his hand was on her mouth again.

"Quiet," he hissed at her and held up the knife, "or I'll stab you again."

Mollie caught her breath, and clamped her mouth shut, looking into his dark eyes. She couldn't make out much detail beyond the mask he wore, but those eyes. Those determined, cold eyes scared her.

She thought about screaming and fighting again. But her eyes caught sight of the knife and the crimson wetness of her blood along the blade.

There'd be other chances.

She nodded and did as he asked.

11

Walking into the office, Jon yawned, still half-asleep. He eyed his office door for a moment, and then thought better of it and walked around to the kitchen instead. He needed caffeine.

Turning into the break room, he spotted Kate pulling some mugs down from the cupboard. He stopped and leant against the door frame, watching her. He'd fallen lucky with this one, he thought. One of his biggest fears, coming down here, was that he'd ended up with a team of people that he either didn't like or respect.

The team you worked with was of paramount importance, and it could have been a disaster. Of course, Damon had reassured him that the team was good and competent. That had given him a modicum of confidence in his choice to move down here, but he couldn't be sure until he'd met them himself.

As it turned out, the team seemed capable and welcoming, so far. Not only that, but he found himself drawn to Kate in ways he'd not been drawn to someone for an awfully long time. She was smart, capable, strong, and she held her own against the boys.

Not only that, but he felt there was something of a kindred spirit in her. She'd had a killer, namely this Abban Devlin guy, take a personal interest in her and try to blackmail her.

It was a little different to his own experience but close enough that he felt she would probably understand what he'd been through. She'd understand what it was like to try and do your job, only for the psychopath you were hunting to turn their eye to you and make you their target.

That was a special kind of terror in that, especially when they hurt someone you loved. As he thought back, images of Charlotte flashed before his eyes. Images of her alive, warm, and vibrant, mixed with hideous visions of her cold, unmoving, and dead.

Those images haunted him still, five years after the fact, and he honestly doubted he'd ever be rid of them.

But in some ways, he didn't want to be free of them. He wanted to remember her no matter what.

"Morning, guv," Kate said.

Snapping out of his reverie, he looked up at her and smiled. "Mornin'."

"Tea?"

"Aye, I'd love a cuppa."

"Coming right up," she replied, and put two teaspoons of loose leaf tea in the teapot, before pouring the freshly boiled water into it. Stirring the beverage, Jon got a whiff of the drink and sighed.

It smelt good.

"You use tea leaves," he commented.

"Of course, you get a much better flavour."

"You think?"

She eyed him. "Are you a bag man, normally?"

"Oh, I love a good tea-bagging," he replied with a wry smile.

Kate raised an eyebrow at him. "I'd beg to differ," she replied and pulled the milk out the fridge. He expected her to just place the container on the counter as they waited for the tea to brew, but instead, she poured some milk into the first mug.

"Whoa! What are you doing?"

She froze and looked up at him. "Um, making tea?"

Jon looked from Kate to the milk, and back up again, his expression expectant, as if it was obvious what he was getting at.

"What?" she asked bewildered.

"You put the milk in first." His voice was incredulous.

"Yeeaah," she replied.

"Why?"

"Because that's how I make tea." Her tone suggested it was the most obvious thing in the world.

"That's not how you make tea. How can you put the milk in first? That's madness."

"No, it's not."

"Yes, it is. You put the tea in first, and then the milk. Not the other way around. Otherwise, how do you know how much milk to put in?"

"I just know. Besides, it tastes better this way."

"What!" Jon couldn't quite believe what he was hearing. How on earth could she think this was how you made tea? This was madness, utter madness. "How on earth does it taste better? It makes no difference, surely. It still mixes together the same."

"Oh, no. I can tell the difference."

"Bullshit."

"No, I bet I can."

"Right, whatever. Give me that milk, missy. I'll show you how to make tea," he started to grumble. "Jeez. Milk in first? I've never heard such craziness."

Reaching for the teapot, he picked it up and went to pour his tea.

"Wait," Kate said.

"What now?"

"You'll need this," she said and handed him the world's smallest sieve. "To catch the tea leaves."

Jon looked at the dinky utensil and shrugged. "Whatever," he muttered and poured the tea into his mug through the sieve. Sure enough, it caught the tea leaves as she'd explained. Replacing the pot, he picked up the milk. "Now, watch and learn," he said. "Look, see. Now I can judge how much milk to put in by the colour of the tea and get it just right. But that," he pointed to her mug, "that is an abomination."

"Right…" Kate replied, drawing the word out.

He smiled at her. "Gather the team, let's get everyone caught up."

Jon walked out of the kitchen, still astonished by Kate's tea-making skills, and into his office to settle in for the day, turn his PC on, and get ready for the morning briefing.

He was halfway through this morning tea, merrily muttering swear words at the computer screen and the endless spam he always seemed to have, when Kate appeared at his door. "Feeling less grumpy now?"

"Nothing like a cuppa to take the edge off."

"Glad to hear it, Mr Tea Nazi."

"Whoa there! Tea Nazi? I think you mean, Tea Angel. I saved you from a fate worse than death."

"Whatever. Did you like the blend?"

"Mmm." Jon nodded. It was lovely. A little different to what he was used to, but there was plenty of flavour in there.

"It's Barry's."

Jon looked up and pulled a quizzical expression. "It's who's now?"

"Barry's Tea."

"And who's Barry when he's at home?"

"No, that's the brand. Barry's Tea. It's Irish, don't yeh know?" Kate's slight Irish brogue came to the fore a little more as she finished her sentence.

"Is it?" He glanced at the remains of the drink, and back up at Kate. "Funny, it doesn't taste like potatoes."

Kate pulled a face and then gave him the finger.

"I'm joking, I'm joking. It's nice. So, are we ready?"

"Yup."

"Then lead on, Barry."

Kate's eyebrows climbed up her forehead. "Oh shit, what have I done?" she muttered as she turned and led him out of the office and into the incident room, where the team was waiting.

"Morning, all," he said, to a round of subdued replies as they all either yawned, shuffled their papers, or waited patiently. Kate took her seat beside him, and Jon sat at the head of the table.

"Right then, updates. Rachel? Any progress?"

"We have a rough route that Harper took on her walk, cobbled together from various eyewitnesses, and some CCTV that caught her. But there are some big gaps in there, with sections where she could have been on three or more roads. We'll keep hunting, but so far, we don't have much more than that."

"Do you think we should go public? Ask for help?"

"Maybe. I can put out a statement, send it to the media along with some CCTV footage."

"Perfect. Get on that."

"Will do, guv."

"Right then, speaking of CCTV, do we have the footage from the camera at Chaucer Gardens?"

"We do," Dion replied, and turned to the large TV on a moveable stand that was at one end of the table. "We've got a pretty good angle on the attackers too," he said and hit play. The image, which was surprisingly good, showed a couple of guys walking along the balcony to the front door of Seth's apartment and knocking. When it opened, the first man surged in through the front door, tackling Tom, and sending him to the floor. The second man stood outside and looked around, including almost directly at the camera. After a moment, he walked inside and closed the door behind him.

He wasn't in there long though, and before long, the pair left the flat and walked away, out of shot.

"So, I took this footage, and some footage from elsewhere on the estate and got the best headshots I could of the two guys and blew them up. They're pretty grainy but better than some of the images I've pulled from CCTV. Now we just need to figure out who they are."

"Great work, Dion. Right, well…"

"Guv," Nathan cut in, peering at the screen. "I think I know that guy who waited outside."

"Oh?"

"That's Dillon Harris, if I'm not mistaken."

Surprised, Jon sat back in his chair. "Are you sure?"

"Pretty sure," Nathan said. "I'd recognise him anywhere."

"And why's that?"

"Because he's a Miller."

"So, he makes bread then, or something? You're going to have to give me more to go on than that, I'm new around here."

"The Millers," Rachel said, nodding sagely now that Nathan had explained things a little more. "They're a gang. A big one. Based in South London."

"They're run by the Miller family, hence the name," Nathan added. "They're powerful and wealthy, but they have a kind of Mafia-like code of honour thing. They don't kill random people or anything. Anyway, I'd bet that the other guy is a Miller too."

"Right," Jon replied, and looked up at the images of the two men again, and grimaced. "So what the hell are they doing beating up Tom?"

"They must have been after Seth," Kate replied.

"Mmmm, yeah," Jon mused. "But why?"

"Don't know, but I'll compare the other guy to the mug shots we've got of the Millers, see if we can get a match."

"I presume we know where these Millers are?"

"The head of the family is called Irving. We know where he lives and he's usually quite happy to help the police out."

"I bet he is," Jon answered. "I wonder how many coppers he has on his payroll?"

Nathan shrugged.

"Alright," Jon replied. "Nathan, do some digging. See what you can find out."

"Will do, guv."

"Okay, so what about Harper's father?"

"Nothing yet," Kate replied. "We tried again this morning, first thing, but no one's answering."

"Great. We need to find him and fast," Jon replied. Kate nodded. "Okay, the cuffs, anything there?"

"Nada," Dion replied. "They're mass-produced with nothing about them we can use to track or identify where they came from, or who bought them. Dead end."

"Wonderful," Jon replied. "Any other links? Did we hunt through the database of police officers, see if there were any links with an officer or ex-officer holding a grudge?"

"The obvious links were to officers who had encounters with Harper or Seth in the past," Kate replied. "But there's nothing there that really stands out as suspect. I'll keep looking, but I'm not hopeful."

The door to the incident room opened and a woman in civilian clothing walked in.

Jon looked up. "Um, a knock would have been nice."

"Sorry," she replied, and Jon felt reasonably sure he'd seen her around the office. She was most likely one of the civilian investigators they used.

"It's alright," Kate said. "Guv, this is Debbie Constable."

Jon glanced at Kate, and then back to Debbie. "Nice name, well done. Excellent choice of job."

"Um, thanks?"

"What is it, Miss Constable?"

"We just had a call. Another body's been found."

12

Jon sat in the passenger seat of the car and let Kate navigate through the winding backroads of the Surrey countryside to the crime scene. She knew her way around here far better than he did and he figured it would just be easier for him to sit this one out.

As Kate drove, Jon scanned through the report.

Someone had found the body in the woods—a dog walker, predictably—and phoned it in. It was a girl strapped to a tree, and the first attending officer reported that she appeared to be missing a couple of fingers on her right hand.

Jon grimaced at that little detail and looked away from the sheet of papers. He'd thought he was getting somewhere yesterday with the investigation. Maybe they had the guy on the ropes and were closing in. But this new development threw doubt on that assumption. Would he really be out there killing again, if he thought he was about to be caught?

"It's definitely another one for us then, it is?" Kate asked.

"Looks that way. Missing fingers and all."

"Damn," she replied. "He's working quick."

They soon found the crime scene. A small crowd of attending police vehicles and officers had taken over a muddy patch of land off the side of the road that served as a car park. The officer at the entrance let them in after checking their IDs.

"So, where are we, exactly?" Jon asked.

"This is Ranmore Common," Kate replied. "We're east of Guildford."

"Right," Jon answered. He was still getting his bearings and only had a rough idea of where he was in the UK.

Getting out, they were soon dressed in their forensic gear and shown along a rough path lined with police tape. Ahead, Jon could see a few people stood around, marking the location of the body a short distance off the beaten path.

"Once more unto the breach, dear friends," Jon remarked as they approached the crime scene. Ahead, Jon could make out that someone who had been attached to a tree, their arms wrapped around it and secured in place by, what Jon was sure would turn out to be, handcuffs.

"It's looking eerily similar," Kate commented.

Walking around to the front, the girl was still dressed, as Harper had been, but wasn't wearing a coat, which Jon noted was discarded a short distance away, and her sleeves had been rolled up. The girl had her back to the tree, her arms pulled behind her around the trunk. She'd slumped as she'd died, her muscles unable to support her weight anymore. Her head hung low, her ginger hair falling about her head, just like Harper's had.

Stood in front of her, an older man held a clipboard and was scribbling on it while a photographer went about his work.

"Morning," the man said in greeting. "Chilly one, isn't it?"

"A little," Jon replied.

"Not too cold, of course, but not warm either. Fresh, I think is the word," the man continued. He had grey, receding hair and wore gold-rimmed glasses and a tweed suit without a tie.

"I'm not sure that's the word I'd use," Jon replied, waving his hand before his nose.

"Hmm? Oh, yes. Very good." He chuckled gently.

"I'm DCI Jon Pilgrim."

"Pat Chambers, police surgeon. A pleasure to meet you."

"Likewise," Jon replied, noting the old term for what was now known as the Forensic Medical Examiner.

"*DS* O'Connell, is it now?"

Kate smiled at him. "That's right, Pat. I got the promotion."

"Well done you. That's great to hear. Well, I can confirm she's dead, for you, so I think that's me done here."

"Excellent work, doctor."

"Indeed. Well, she's all yours. Looks like you have a serial on your hands. Hope you get him quick if this is the rate he's offing them. See you later."

Jon bid the man goodbye, as Sheridan walked through to join them with a couple of other SOCOs right behind her.

"You beat me to it," Sheridan said.

"Just trying to keep you on your toes," Jon replied.

"Looks like it might be the same killer as yesterday," Kate added.

"Wonderful," Sheridan muttered as she peered at the corpse. "Jeez, poor thing. She looks young."

Jon nodded.

"She does," Kate agreed.

"Right, let's have a look, shall we?" Stepping closer, Sheridan went to work, examining the girl and the scene, and assigning tasks to her colleagues. Jon moved around the victim, looking at her from every angle, looking for bruises, marks, and other hints for what had happened to her. On the back of the tree, as he expected, the girl's hands had been secured with a pair of metal handcuffs that glinted in the morning light. They were partially covered with blood, from the obvious and painfully deep cuts on both forearms.

As with Harper, she was also missing two fingers on her right hand. The pinkie and ring finger, just as Harper had been.

"It's the same MO," Jon muttered. "Wrists slashed, cuffs, and fingers missing."

Sheridan, who was crouched down beside the tree, looked up. "No, they're here. Discarded, like with Harper." She pointed to the two severed digits that lay in the grass and mud at the base of the tree. "I wonder why he doesn't take them or do anything with them?"

"Because the act of removing them is the message, not the digits themselves," Jon replied. "Once they're removed, the severed fingers have no value."

"I think you need to work out what message he's trying to send," Sheridan said. "I spoke with the pathologist yesterday after she'd examined the body. It looks like the fingers were removed by bolt cutters or shears."

"Ouch," Jon remarked, flexing his fingers as he imagined what that must feel like.

"Yeah, pretty nasty."

Jon nodded and looked over to where Kate crouched a few metres away near the coat. "Anything?" he asked.

"I've got her coat, gloves, and her purse," Kate replied. "We have a student ID card here, too. It belongs to a Mollie Hayes, a student at Surrey University in Guildford, according to this. She was carrying a bit of cash too. I think about seventy-five pounds?"

"A student? Hmm. No obvious link to Harper then."

"Nothing that stands out," Kate replied. "But it looks like we'll have no issue identifying her and finding her family. I'll get this called in and get Faith to head on over to her parents."

"Good call," Jon replied. "We'll need to inform the university, too."

With a sigh, Jon stepped away from the tree and moved a few metres away, before he turned and took a long look at the scene, trying to get a wider view, and wondering what the killer was trying to tell them.

Two girls, both young, killed through blood loss and missing two fingers—the pattern was clear, but what was he trying to tell them? Why was he doing this? It felt like someone was shouting at him but in a foreign language. He just didn't understand what the killer was trying to tell them.

Looking around, he wondered about the location of the murder too. Was this wood important somehow? It was isolated and quiet, like the factory, but maybe there was more to it than that, but if so, what?

Things were not looking good, and time was passing. Would there be another body tomorrow?

He hoped not. All they could do was follow the clues and hope for some kind of breakthrough.

13

"So, did you get out for that drink with Damon, last night?" Kate asked as she drove towards Guildford and Mollie's family's home.

"I did," Jon replied with a smile as he thought back to the visit to the local pub.

"You weren't too worse for wear then this morning?"

"Nah. It wasn't a heavy one. We just had a couple of pints and talked about our time back on the Nottingham force together. We had some good times."

"And then he joined the National Crime Agency?"

"Yeah. Damon was an intelligent guy. Studied ancient history, theology, and mythology. He was always into that kind of stuff, and the NCA liked his insight into some fairly high profile cases and asked if he wanted to join them as a specialist. He's been with them ever since."

"Ah, sounds like someone else I know."

"Oh?"

"Nathan's kind of like that, but in a more, Fox Mulder kind of way."

"The nickname," Jon replied, making the connection.

Kate nodded. "He was always a bit of a conspiracy nut, apparently. Thought that there were these hidden groups, influencing society or government or just out to enrich themselves. But it started affecting his work."

"I'm guessing that didn't go well for him?"

"No," Kate said, shaking her head. "He used to be a DCI. Bit of a hotshot by the sounds of things, but then he seriously screwed up a case because he was obsessed with his conspiracy theories and got demoted."

"Looks like he's working his way back up, though."

"Yeah. When I joined the Murder Team, he was just a DS, and basically shunned by the others. They used him as a hazing ritual for new officers, by partnering them up with him to see how they did. Thing was, I kind of liked working with him, and as it turned out, at least in one respect, he was right. Nathan and I were tracking a group of wealthy people who appear to be part of a group, a bit like a cult. They'd been killing people for who knew what reason and Mr Devlin was the last one of the group we caught."

"Wow, that's crazy. So you took the group down?"

"No, I don't think so. But I think we put a sizable dent in their operation. We've not heard from them in a while. Anyway, it was through our investigation into that group that we met Damon."

"I see. I wondered how Damon had gotten involved with you all."

"Well, now you know."

Jon nodded.

They made their way into one of the wealthy suburbs of Guildford, filled with large, well-kept houses with lots of garden space. This was a world away from the Sutton flat of Seth Bailey, and even from Iris Richards' council estate house. Mollie's parents were obviously well off.

"This is all very nice," Jon replied as he marvelled at the inviting houses. "Which reminds me, I need to find a place of my own."

"Where are you staying right now?" Kate asked.

"Premier Inn, Guildford. All my stuff's in storage locally."

"Yeah, you need a place of your own."

"I wonder if I could afford a house like these?"

Kate laughed. "On a police salary? Not likely."

"Figures," Jon grumbled as Kate pulled in and parked up behind DC Faith Evenson's car. "Let's go and have a look inside, so I can get nicely depressed and lament my career choices."

"Sounds like a solid plan," Kate answered.

"Lead on then, Barry."

Kate paused and looked over at him with a raised eyebrow. "That's my nickname from now on, isn't it?"

Jon raised his hands in surrender. "Hey, I didn't choose the tea."

She sighed. "Alright, Pilgrim. Let's go."

Jon nodded, followed Kate up the driveway to the house, and rang the doorbell. Faith answered and stepped outside.

"Guv, Kate," she greeted them. "As you'd expect, they're a mess, but they're ready to answer your questions."

"Good," Jon replied.

"So, this is the same guy who killed Harper, is it?"

"Almost without a doubt," he answered. "And if we don't find him, I doubt it will be his last either."

Faith nodded. "You'd better come in then," she suggested and led them into the house. They found the parents in the living room, along with a teenager who was snuggled up to the mother. All their eyes were red, tissues littered the coffee table and the floor, and the haunted looks on their faces told him everything he needed to know about how this had already affected them.

This family would never be the same again.

He'd seen it happen many times over the years when someone was killed or some other huge trauma had impacted a family. Some pulled together and forged on, using the event as a way to grow and become stronger. Others, however, didn't fare quite so well. If the relationships weren't strong, events like this only widened those cracks and fractured the family.

He wondered how the Hayes would fare.

"Okay then, introductions," Faith began as she stood to one side. "This is DCI Jon Pilgrim and DS Kate O'Connell. They'll be leading the investigation."

Jon nodded as they looked up at them. "I'm sorry for your loss," he said.

The man stood and stepped up to him, holding his hand out. "Oliver Hayes, Mollie's dad," he said. Jon could hear the slight crack in his voice as he held his emotion in check as best he could. "This is my wife, Daphne, and my younger daughter, Flora."

"Hello," Jon said. He chose his words carefully. His instinct would usually push him to say something like, 'nice to meet you,' but he often felt such words were inappropriate during these times. Sure, it might be pleasant to meet new people, but this family was in shock and grieving, and he didn't want to upset them.

"Please, take a seat," Oliver suggested after greeting Kate as well. He took his place beside his wife and put his arm around her. He made sure his wife was ok with a quick whisper, before looking over at Jon and Kate with an expectant look on his face. Daphne looked up too and waited.

"I'm sorry for the terrible news today," Jon began. "I know this must be a living nightmare for you right now, but we need to ask you some questions so that, hopefully, we can find the man who did this to your daughter."

"You're sure it's her?" Daphne blurted out. "You're sure it's Mollie?"

"We're very sure," he replied. We're still waiting on a primary identifier, which I think will be dental records, but she'd been carrying her photo ID on her at the time, which all seems to match. Also, the university has confirmed she's not there. She went out last night and never came back."

Daphne whimpered, and Flora sobbed.

"Can you tell us about her?" Kate asked.

"She was a wonderful girl," Oliver replied. "Just such a lovely young woman. She had her whole life ahead of her. Why would anyone want to do this to her?"

"That's what we will endeavour to find out," Jon replied.

"So, she was at university?" Kate asked.

"Studying Law," Oliver replied. Jon picked up a note of pride in her father's voice.

"And you don't know any reason why someone would want to do this to her?"

"None," Oliver replied.

"No, of course not," Daphne added. "She was always good with people. She's got some great friends. I can't think of anyone or any reason why someone would want to murder my baby." Daphne's voice broke as she came to the end of the sentence.

Beside her, Oliver pulled her close, and all three remaining members of the family supported each other. It was heart-wrenching to see, but there was a good, loving relationship there, which gave Jon hope that they would get through this with each other's support.

Jon and Kate continued to ask questions, finding out a bit more about Mollie's life, but there was little there in terms of anything suspicious. She was popular, a diligent student, and had a supportive family without anything that would typically give Jon pause.

As he walked out of the house, Jon felt bewildered and a little lost.

"I might be missing something obvious here, but there really wasn't anything there, was there?"

"No, you're right," Kate replied. "She seems well-liked and loved, and at least at first glance, there doesn't seem to be any link to Harper."

"That's what I thought. Shit. Now what?"

14

Jon watched the girl walk in and approach Kate.

"Rupa, thanks for talking to us," Kate said, shaking her hand, and placing her other on the back of it. She gave Rupa a reassuring smile. She looked emotionally drained, with puffy eyes that glistened with tears yet to fall.

Watching Kate with the girl and how dedicated to the job she was, he couldn't quite believe that he'd considered taking her off the case yesterday.

Kate was professional and dogged in her hunt for this killer, as he'd hoped and expected her to be. Clearly, he'd been a little rash in his thinking, and although he'd not acted on it, he felt bad that he'd considered it at all.

Right now, he couldn't think of anyone else he'd rather have by his side on this case.

Having greeted Kate, Rupa looked up at Jon and shook his hand too.

"You have my condolences," Jon said.

"Thank you."

"How are you holding up?" Kate asked.

"I'm alright, I suppose. All things considered. I just can't believe she's gone. She was my best friend." She pulled out a tissue and dabbed at the tears that had formed in her eyes.

"If there's anything I can do to help you find the killer, please, just ask."

"Well, *you* were her best friend, according to her parents and the staff here," Jon said. "Can you think of any reason why someone would do this to her? Anything at all?"

"Spurned advances by a guy?" Kate added. "Jealousy from a peer? Anything?"

"No, absolutely not," Rupa replied. "You didn't know Mollie. She was just the loveliest girl you've ever met. She'd do anything for anyone. Everyone liked her. Like, everyone. I don't know anyone who'd say a bad word about her."

"You're sure?" Kate pressed.

"Positive. Just ask anyone."

"We are doing," Jon replied. He'd already brought Rachel and Nathan over to help with the seemingly endless list of people to interview. He and Kate had spoken to several members of staff before her friends had been brought in, and it seemed that everyone's opinion was universally positive. Not only that, from what he could tell from the records of the classes she took, and her friends and their families, no one had an obvious link to Harper or Seth.

Just one more dead-end in a seemingly endless series of them.

"Okay, so tell me what you know about what happened last night," Jon asked.

"We'd planned to hang out," Rupa replied.

"Who had?"

"Me, Mollie, and Brad. We were going to meet up in Mollie's room and just... chill, you know?"

"Chill? What do you mean by 'chill', exactly?"

"What? Well, I... Oh, you mean...? No! Not that," Rupa replied. "We're just friends. We'd have a few drinks and stuff, chat, maybe watch a film. Nothing very exciting. We've all got a load of work on from our courses, so we don't get out as much as we used to."

"Okay, but at some point, Mollie went out. Do you know why?"

"Supply run, probably?" Rupa shrugged. "I didn't even know she'd gone. I had work to catch up on."

"What kind of supplies?"

"I don't know."

"She had seventy-five pounds on her, that's quite a lot for a student," Kate pressed.

Rupa flushed slightly. "We all pitched in earlier on. Mollie offered to go buy some stuff because she had less work to do last night."

"So, she was just getting drinks and snacks then, nothing else?" Jon asked.

"I don't think so," Rupa replied. She didn't seem to know where to look, as her eyes darted around the room.

"You're sure?"

"As far as I know," Rupa replied.

Jon wasn't convinced, but couldn't be sure she was lying. Maybe she was just nervous about being questioned. They threw a bunch more questions at her, jumping between her relationship with Mollie and the events of last night, and anything else they could think of, but her story never wavered.

In the end, they let her go and brought in Mollie's other close friend, Bradley, and asked many of the same questions again.

"So, what about your relationship with Mollie?" Kate asked. "What can you tell us?"

"She's a friend. A really great friend... or was, I guess." He looked crestfallen and broken.

"And that's all it was?" Jon asked. "You were just friends?"

"Oh, yeah," Bradley replied. He was a skinny guy, and like Rupa, seemed deflated by his friend's death. "I mean, she's nice and all, but I didn't fancy her or anything. We just hung out. We were friends."

"And as a friend, you let her go out on her own to buy... whatever, for your meet-up last night?"

"She wanted to do it. She's done it before and been fine."

"But she wasn't yesterday, was she?"

"How was I supposed to know what would happen?" he protested, a sudden fire behind his words. "I didn't want anything to happen to her. I'd do anything to change things, to bring her back."

"That's okay," Kate cut in. "We know you would, but we need to know everything that happened."

"I wish I could help you, I really do. But I was working when she went to the shops."

"To get supplies?"

"That's right."

"So, drinks and snacks?"

"I think so," Bradley replied. He was sitting very still and was making a point of looking Jon in the eyes as he spoke.

"So, nothing else. Nothing a little harder, maybe?"

"You mean drugs."

"I didn't say that," Jon replied.

"You didn't need to."

"Well, did she?"

"I don't think so."

"You're sure," Jon pressed.

Bradley nodded, a little too vigorously.

"What do you know about the money she was carrying?"

"We gave Mollie some cash," he replied without missing a beat.

They were all the same answers as Rupa gave. Answers that could be true, but he wasn't entirely convinced. It all felt a little fishy to Jon, like they were holding something back, despite their protestations.

The interview dragged on, followed by others with Mollie's less close friends until they had little choice but to end it for the day. They'd need someone to come back tomorrow and work through the people who were left on the list, but for now, they were done, and Jon was feeling more than a little frustrated by the complete lack of leads.

Why Mollie? Why kill her? What was the link between her and Harper? Did the killer know them or pick them at random? Because right now, there seemed little rhyme or reason to the killer's choices.

"Did you believe them?" Jon asked.

"Her friends?" Kate asked. "I don't know. I take it you didn't, though."

"Something didn't feel right. I think they were lying about why Mollie went out."

"So, why do *you* think she went out? To buy drugs?"

"Is that so strange?"

Kate sighed. "No. I guess not. I think most people experiment a little bit during their teenage years and early twenties, don't you?"

Jon nodded, remembering his own teenage rebellion. He remembered hating that his dad was a police officer for a short time while at school. Some cruel classmates seemed to think that was a bad thing and Jon had hated that. So he rebelled. He drank while underage, smoked weed, he'd even given a couple of the more serious drugs a try, but luckily never got hooked on anything.

He'd been a stupid kid, not that he'd thought that at the time, but looking back, it was so clear to him.

"Yeah," Kate replied. "I tried a few things back then too. They probably think they're going to get into trouble."

"Yeah, probably. Aaah well, we'll talk to them again tomorrow, and see what we can get out of them."

"Good plan," Kate stood and stretched. "Right, what are you doing now then?"

Jon shrugged. Gonna go home, get some kip, and come back in tomorrow so I can do it all over again."

"Home?" Kate asked.

"Heh. Well, back to my room at the hotel. What about you?"

"I don't know. I guess I could collapse in front of the TV with a ready meal. And yes, I do live an exciting life."

"Aww, don't. You're making me jealous."

Kate laughed. "Oh, I know. I'm living the high life right here."

"So, where do you live then? Where's home for you?"

"Just a dingy little flat in Leatherhead. It's nothing special."

"That's a really strange name for a town, don't you think? Leatherhead?"

"A bit, I suppose. I've not really thought about it before."

"Sounds like some kind of serial killer name."

"You're thinking of Leatherface, from The Texas Chainsaw Massacre."

"Hah, yeah, I suppose. So there's no garden-tool-wielding psychos in town, then?"

Kate laughed. "Heh, no. Well, not that I've seen so far, anyway."

They'd left the room and were walking back to the car as they spoke. Jon stepped up to the passenger-side door and waited for Kate to unlock it. She paused on the other side, pulled a face, and then looked up at him.

"Do you want to get a drink?"

"Um," Jon replied, thinking about it for a moment, and then shrugged and smiled. "Yeah, sure. Sounds good."

15

After dropping off their notes at the station, Jon closed his office door and looked over at Kate where she stood before her PC, leaning over to turn it off, and felt a moment of guilt run through his mind.

Was this the right thing to do? Should he really be doing this?

He wondered what Charlotte would think of him going for a drink with his female partner. He couldn't help but feel guilty, as though he was cheating on her somehow, even though she'd been gone for five years now.

But then, this wasn't his first dalliance with a woman since his wife had passed. He'd had a few dates and encounters over the last few years. Nothing that lasted very long though.

Usually, he ended things because he felt like he was cheating on Charlotte, or *they* left *him* because they didn't like the photos of Charlotte at his home. That, or they just couldn't cope with his dedication to the job and the long hours that inevitably came with it.

He wasn't sure this was even a date though, not really. He didn't want to assume anything and thought it best to think of it as nothing more than a quick drink with a work friend. Like he'd done with Damon last night.

He couldn't help how his eyes were drawn to her, however, as he watched her finish up at her computer and then walk over, smiling at him as she pulled on her magenta coat.

"Ready?" she asked.

"Of course," he replied, and followed her out of the station. "Do you think anything will come from these chats with Mollie's friends?"

Kate smiled. "I have no idea," she said. "Who knows. Maybe."

"Yeah, maybe..."

"Tell you what, no work talk tonight," she said.

Jon met her gaze and then nodded. "Yeah, okay. That'll be a challenge."

"How come?"

"That's about all I've done for the last five years. Eat, sleep, and work."

"I'm sure there's more to you than that, Pilgrim."

"If there is, I don't know what it could be. I'm a fairly one-dimensional kind of man."

"Aren't all men that shallow?"

"Oh, wow. We're going there are we, Barry?"

"If you're going to insist on calling me Barry, then yeah, we're going there," she replied as they walked out of the station.

"Alright, point taken."

"So, what do you think of her then?"

"Who?"

"The station." Kate pointed back at the brutalist grey building.

"Well, I guess she's alright. Certainly better appointed than my previous station."

"Yeah, she does us proud."

Jon nodded as they spotted a gap in the traffic and crossed the road.

"Oh, look, they knew you were coming," he said and pointed to the stocks that were on a patch of grass in front of the establishment.

"I think they'd suit you better. I could do with some target practice. Why don't you pop your head in there, and I'll find some tomatoes to chuck at you."

"You just want to have your wicked way with me, don't you, Miss O'Connell?"

"How did you guess? Shit, I'm going to have to watch what I say from now on," she quipped, as they walked into the pub, and over to the bar.

"I'll buy," Jon said.

"Fair enough. I'll get the next round."

"You're planning on talking to me for that long?"

"Depends on if you send me to sleep or not, Pilgrim."

"Moi? Send you to sleep? No way. I'll give you a pinch every now and then to make sure you're still awake."

"Promises, promises."

"What are you having?"

Kate thought for a moment before answering. "Just a glass of red, I think. You?"

"Well, I've gotta drive back so, a shandy will do me for now."

Kate nodded, and he ordered their drinks before they wandered through the pub and found a table and some comfortable chairs towards the back.

"So, what do you do with yourself when you're not arresting people?" she asked.

"Not a lot," he replied. "You know what it's like. It's not as if we have that much free time, and I've pretty much thrown myself into my work these days. But, you said no work talk I guess so…"

"Okay, let's clarify. No talk about this current case. I'd like to get away from that for a few hours."

Jon nodded. "Fair enough."

"So, you don't do anything else?"

Jon smiled and chuckled to himself. "Well, no. I enjoy watching films. I've got quite the collection in storage."

"Alright," she replied. "There you go, you see, you do have some interests outside of work. So, what do you tend to watch?"

"I tend to like science-fiction and stuff. I don't tend to watch thrillers or crime dramas."

"Too close to home?"

Jon nodded. "I want my films to be escapism. I don't want to end up analysing a film and criticising it for being inaccurate or anything, you know? If I'm watching a film, I want to be taken on a journey, and get away from the horrors of this job and the world."

"I know the feeling. I'll watch most things, but I tend to steer away from police stuff usually."

"What about you? What do you do to get away from it all?" Jon asked. "Do you have any hobbies?"

"Me?" Kate smiled. "Well, I enjoy a bit of photography."

"Photography? Really? Wow, that's great. I didn't expect that."

"I'm full of surprises," she replied with a coy smile.

"So, what kind of photography?"

"Just landscapes, mainly. I used to go to a local photography club, but I just couldn't get there most weeks because of work, so I gave that up. These days I usually like to go on long walks with my camera, and if I see something good, then I'll snap a photo."

"I'd love to see some of your work."

"No, you wouldn't. I'm not very good. I just do it for myself, really."

"I'll bet you're better than you think you are."

She blushed and brushed him off "No, seriously, I just do it for myself. I'm not amazing or anything."

"So you never wanted to be a forensic photographer?"

"Ugh, no. That's not my thing at all."

"You'd get to work with some very compliant models though. They'd never complain."

"Yeah, that's because the models are dead," Kate laughed.

Jon laughed with her, having completely forgotten about his feelings of guilt. Instead, he just enjoyed Kate's company.

16

Finally, Emily thought, stepping out of the back of the shop and letting the door slam home none-too-carefully. She didn't care, she just wanted to get home. She'd worked so much later than she'd hoped, and had her doubts she'd make it home in time.

But, there was a silver lining in there. The extra hours were always useful.

Just think of the money, she thought. That's why she was doing this. It would all be worth it in the end.

As she strode along the back road and out to a main high street in Redhill, she rifled through her bag until she felt the smooth, hard surface of her phone and pulled it out. Waking it up, she saw a slew of messages from Morgan and cursed silently. She'd missed his calls.

Choosing not to read them, she went straight to calling him instead. He picked up after a few rings.

"Hiya."

"Hey," she replied as she walked.

"There you are. I was beginning to wonder if they'd ever let you go."

"Yeah, I know. Sorry about that. They needed me to put in a few more hours, and I just didn't have the time to call you. I hope you don't mind?"

"Yeah, it's fine."

"Are you sure?"

"Of course," he answered, his voice calm and reassuring. "It's all money in the wedding fund at the end of the day, yeah?"

"I know, I know. I just feel bad for not getting home in time to see you before you leave. Have you set off yet?"

"Just about to."

"Shit, sorry. I just wanted to catch you before you left."

"I know. It's okay," he reassured her. "I'll see you when I'm back, okay?"

"Yeah, I know. I don't like it when you go away." She hated it, in fact. The lonely house, the empty bed. She always felt so much more vulnerable. Just walking back to the car tonight, knowing she'd be returning to an empty house gave her the creeps.

"Think of the money. Just focus on that."

"I know, I will. It'll be worth it."

"Of course it will," he replied. "You're going to try on your wedding dress again at the weekend, right?"

"Yeah. I can't wait."

"I'm looking forward to seeing you in it."

"I bet."

"...and taking you out of it again," he added, saucily.

"I think you'll find that's not as easy as you think."

"Then I won't take it off, you can leave it on while we..."

"Morgan! Jeez, what's got into you?" She rolled her eyes.

"I just miss you, babe. We seem to be like ships passing in the night, right now. I hardly see you."

"I know," she lamented, with a drawn-out sigh. "I hate it too. I'll make it up to you, I promise."

"That would be good. I know a way you can make it up to me, by the way."

She raised an eyebrow, having a fairly good idea of what was coming. "Go on then," she replied.

"You could wear that lingerie I bought you, maybe?"

"You really do have a one-track mind, don't you?" She didn't mind, not really, and kind of enjoyed him taking such an interest in her.

"Absence makes the heart grow fonder..."

"And the dick harder?"

Morgan laughed. "Don't, I might never go on this trip if you keep talking to me like that."

"Oh really? Is that so? Maybe I should start talking dirty to you more often then? Or send some photos of me wearing that frankly scandalous underwear you gave me."

"Emily, shit. Now I want to stay home and wait for you to get back here."

She laughed. "Don't be stupid. Go on, get going. You don't want to lose your job over your overactive libido."

"Yeah, I know. I'll see you tomorrow night then, okay?"

"You will. Call me, yeah?"

"I will. Drive safely. Love you."

"Love you too. Bye." She hung up, smiling, but already missing him. It was for the best, and the bonus he got from making this trip, plus how good it looked to the company was totally worth it.

It would all pay off in the end, and then they could hopefully spend a little more time together.

Emily continued up the street, past the bus stop, and could see the car park on her right, over the road. She looked behind her to check for a gap in traffic, but there wasn't one right at that moment. So she kept going, and as she glanced back again a few moments later, she spotted a man who was walking up behind her. She couldn't get a good look at his face, but for a moment she thought he was heading right for her. A frown creased her forehead, but she shook it off. It's just my imagination, she thought.

As she walked, she suddenly spotted a break in the traffic up ahead. Checking behind her again, she saw the man striding after her. Or was he just walking on the same side of the road? The road was quiet the other way too, so she veered right and crossed at a jog.

Her car was not far ahead. She'd soon be there and safe.

Now on the other side of the road, she glanced back and suddenly spotted the man making the same crossing. That felt suspicious. Why would he do that?

Emily pushed on, picking up speed, and deciding to not look behind her in case she drew his attention too much.

Or, maybe that was what she should do? Maybe if she showed him that she was onto him, he'd rethink what he was doing and leave her alone.

Turning right into the car park, she looked back up the road and gave him a none too subtle stare, but he didn't seem to register it at all.

Well, she wasn't about to stand here and wait for him. Emily walked into the car park and threaded her way through the few remaining vehicles that were left this late at night.

Hers was a little deeper in, and she soon spotted it and pulled her keys out. The moment she knew she was in range, she started pressing the button on the key fob, unlocking the car, ready for a swift entrance. As she closed the last few metres to the driver's side door, she decided to have one last check behind her.

He was much closer and heading right for her. There was no doubt in her mind now that he was following her. There was nothing else that he would be interested in.

Without thinking, she covered the last few metres in a jog.

Had he called out?

She missed it. What had he said?

Pulling the door open, she jumped in, hitting the lock button as quickly as she could and jamming the keys into the ignition. It took her three tries to insert it, and as the keys slid home, the man reached her window…

…and knocked.

She looked up.

The man sported greying hair and a smile and was holding up one of her gloves.

"You dropped this."

Emily blinked, and for a long moment, found herself unable to breathe. Then she suddenly released the breath and gasped as relief flooded through her body. She couldn't help but laugh.

"Sorry, didn't mean to startle you," the man said. "I'm not quite the spring chicken I used to be and couldn't catch you up."

Emily rolled down her window a few inches, and he slipped the glove through the gap.

"Thank you, I'm sorry," she said.

"That's okay. Have a nice evening," he said, and with a friendly smile, doffed his cap and walked off.

Emily watching him go and shook her head as he disappeared beyond a car and a white van.

She'd been silly. But she guessed it was better to be safe than sorry. She'd never been seriously stalked but had dealt with unwanted comments from men several times in her life. She'd just always tried to be careful, to watch her surroundings, and be aware of people around her.

Occasionally she got spooked at something totally innocent, but she guessed that was better than the alternative.

As her heart slowed and returned to a more regular speed, she set off, driving out the car park and heading home. She put the radio on and turned it up in an effort to take her mind off things as she went.

Reaching her road, she pulled in and got out of the car. The street was dark and quiet, the street lamps casting a dull glow over the scene as she walked the few metres to her home.

She still couldn't believe how stupid she'd been. How could she not have realised that he was harmless, and was just trying to return her property?

She shook her head as she fiddled with her keys and stepped up to her front door. It unlocked easily, and as she stepped inside, she heard something behind her. A rapid-fire thunder of feet on concrete as a shadow lunged for her. He tackled her through the doorway. The attacker's weight threw her to the floor with a thud, knocking the breath right out of her.

Winded, she gasped, struggling for a breath that wouldn't come. His hand held her by the throat as she panicked, sucking in air, and trying to get her lungs to work properly. She was dimly aware of her door being slammed shut and the shadowy man placing his two hands around her throat.

Just as her lungs decided they wanted to breathe again, she found she couldn't. His grip wouldn't let her. She tried to fight, to push him off. But she had no strength left, and she succumbed quickly to the darkness and the sweet embrace of oblivion.

17

Sitting up in bed, Jon wiped the sleep from his eyes and stretched, before leaning back on his headboard and thinking back to the incredibly pleasant evening he'd spent with Kate in the pub.

Fun was probably the word he'd use to describe his feelings towards the evening.

He'd actually had a fun night.

Kate was great company and he'd found her engaging with a keen wit that he appreciated. Also, it was good to get away from the working day and the stresses that the case brought with it.

Telling people that their child has been killed was horrific and never got easier, so being able to step away from that, and have a normal evening, talking about more everyday things, was a blessing.

Plus, Kate was great company.

He liked her.

Quite a lot.

Shaking his head, Jon tried to banish those thoughts. He wasn't sure if it was appropriate for him to be looking at someone on his team in that way. Plus, there was his ever-present guilt to deal with as well.

He knew the rules regarding relationships within the police. They weren't banned by any stretch, and in fact, dating someone who knew the demands and stresses of the job could actually be beneficial. The main thing was that any relationship should not compromise the police or their ability to properly investigate a case or do their job.

Her being his subordinate might be an issue, and might cause those higher up to consider moving one of them, but it might also be fine.

It wouldn't be for him to decide anyway. Besides, it was far too early to be thinking of such things. Premature, in fact, given that nothing had actually happened.

No, Jon's larger issue was his feelings, and as his mind drifted back to Charlotte, he wondered how she'd have felt about it. He'd never had a chance to talk to her about this kind of thing. There was no warning that her end was fast approaching.

She'd been cruelly stolen from him by that bastard who had, in turn, changed Jon's life forever.

He would never be the same again, not least in the way he thought about other women and the idea of being with anyone else. Charlotte had been his life. She'd been amazing and he'd loved her with every fibre of his being. Was there anyone else out there like her? Would he ever find someone who could match up to who she'd been?

He honestly had his doubts that he'd ever be able to find a love like that again, and yet, he also knew it was possible, and that he was just thinking about it wrong.

He wasn't replacing Charlotte. She'd still be there in his memories. She'd helped shape him into the man he was today, and no one could ever take that from him. It was more about him just moving on and living his life. Charlotte would never want him to be miserable. She'd not want him to live the rest of his life alone, either.

She'd want him to be happy, to find love, and family. That's what she'd want.

But would Kate be interested in him? Most likely not. He was a mess, after all, and several years older than her. She probably wouldn't want someone with his baggage, either.

Who would?

With a grunt, Jon got up, got dressed, and headed downstairs to partake in the wonders of the hotel breakfast, again lamenting that there was no black pudding in the delicacies that were on offer. He'd asked, but for whatever reason—and he'd not really gotten a clear reason why—it just wasn't on the menu at this time.

A small part of him wanted to head to a local butcher so he could bring it in himself, but there was a far larger part of him that told him not to be such a prick.

Suck it up, Pilgrim.

Besides, once he got a place of his own, it would most likely be a quick bowl of cereal in the morning rather than the belt-busting, fat-filled, heart attack on a plate that this was.

Just enjoy it while you can.

In short order, Jon was out of the hotel and heading east towards the station, cursing the traffic as he went, and feeling smugly superior to the queues crawling into town going the other way.

Walking into the office, Jon looked left over the array of desks and workstations, wondering if Kate or any of the others would be there. He spotted Nathan, who always seemed to be in early, as well as Dion who was hunkered down at his machine, but no Kate. Was she not in yet? Had he scared her off?

But as he walked, Kate wandered out of the break room with a morning tea. She spotted him, and Jon felt a flush of blood rush through him on seeing her.

She smiled and pointed to the mug in her hand. "Want one?"

"Sure," he replied with a nod. "That would be lovely."

"Won't be a moment, kettle's boiled," she replied as she placed the mug she was holding beside Nathan.

Jon smiled and walked into his private office, only to pause and remember how Kate actually made tea.

He rolled his eyes with a sigh, but then shrugged.

Whatever.

Jon dumped his stuff, firing up the PC, and starting to go through the case in his head again. They were no closer to catching this guy. Yesterday's new body had led them to focus on questioning the seemingly endless numbers of students that knew Mollie, rather than on Harper and the links she had to the criminal community. The issue being that Harper's circle of friends seemed like a much richer environment for finding someone capable of committing these murders, but things could be deceptive and were often never what they first appeared to be.

And then there was the nagging worry that it had been another day, and if the killer kept up this same pattern of behaviour, there might be another body out there somewhere, waiting for someone to find it.

Shit, it all felt like such a mess, and after such a promising start that first day.

"Hey there," Kate said as she walked in. Jon noticed she was wearing a knee-length skirt today, rather than trousers, and found his eyes drawn to her shape briefly, before pulling them away and smiling at her.

"Thanks." He accepted the tea and eyed the liquid within critically. "So, did you…"

"My tea making skills are perfectly acceptable, but if you want to get up off yeh arse and make your own tea, be my guest, but that's all I'm giving you."

"Fair point." Jon smiled. "Thanks for last night."

She visibly relaxed. "No problem."

"It's exactly what I needed, I think. Just to do something normal, you know?"

"Yeah," she replied with a smile. "I know. It's good to just get away from all this… right?"

He nodded. "The good company helped too," he added and looked up at her over his mug as he took a sip.

He felt sure he caught the briefest flash of embarrassment from her, just a hint of a flush as she smiled back. "It was good to talk to you too, just person to person, you know, and not DCI to DS."

He nodded.

"If you want some normality again sometime…" She smiled at him.

"I'll keep that in mind," he replied.

She nodded, turned to walk away, only to stop in the doorway and look back. "Briefing shortly?"

"You read my mind. Get the team together. I'll be out in a mo."

She nodded and winked before stepping out. Jon watched her go, feeling his heart thud in his chest as she disappeared from view.

Was she flirting with him? He felt like she was, but couldn't be certain of it. He did his best to banish those thoughts from his mind, though. The last thing he needed was to become distracted at this stage in the case.

This was probably what the guidelines on relationships were meant for, to keep this kind of thing from happening and impacting investigations.

A short time later, as Jon was finishing up his morning check on his emails, Nathan appeared at his door.

"I think we're ready for you," he said.

"Oh, crap, yeah," he said and got up. "Sorry, got bogged down in emailing the Nigerian prince who wants to send me his fortune."

Nathan smirked. "That was last month's scam, I think."

"Yeah, and next months," Jon replied as he gathered his folder.

"So," Nathan said, "how was your date?"

Jon froze, and then looked up. "My what?"

"You went to the pub with Irish last night. How was it?"

Jon tilted his head. "I'm not sure it was a date, exactly."

"Are you sure?"

"I, um..." Jon's mind raced as he thought things through, and as much as he had thought it might have been one, he hesitated to call it that. "Did she say that to you?"

Nathan grimaced. "She didn't have to. I can tell."

"How?"

"Well, for one, she's never worn a skirt to work before."

"Oh, well, I'm not sure what that tells you. Maybe her other stuff's in the wash? But our *evening* at the pub was very nice, thank you," Jon replied, choosing his words carefully.

Nathan smiled briefly as Jon picked up his things and moved towards the door.

"Good," Nathan replied, his tone becoming serious as he moved in front of Jon. "I wouldn't want her to get hurt." His tone was full of menace and implication.

Stopping, Jon eyed Nathan. "What are you implying?"

"Nothing."

"Good. Because I wouldn't *want* to hurt her, not that anything is happening between us, or that it's any of your business, frankly. So step away, DI Halliwell."

Nathan sighed, and Jon could see the confrontation within him die away.

"Sorry, guv. I just... I worry about her. She's been through a lot recently and I just don't want to see her get hurt."

"I understand that, but the drinks were entirely innocent."

"Sure."

"I don't want to see anyone on my team get hurt, just in case that wasn't clear. I understand that Kate had a close encounter with Mr Devlin kidnapping her neighbour, and I wouldn't want any of you to have something like that happen." As he spoke, those same horrific memories of Charlotte flashed in his mind.

He wouldn't wish that on anyone, least of all Kate or any other member of this team.

"Yeah, well, there's a little more to it than that, but that's for her to tell you, not me."

"Oh? Yeah, sure. I guess." More to it? What more could there be? Had she been through something similar to him?

"Come on, guys, hurry it up," Rachel called out across the room from the entrance of the incident room.

"Sorry, guv," Nathan said.

"It's already forgotten."

Nathan nodded and walked over to the incident room to join the others who were sat around the table waiting for them.

"Right then, so what have we got?" Jon began as he placed his folder down on the desk and took his seat. "Two victims, Mollie Hayes and Harper Richards, both killed in the exact same way, right?" Jon looked over at Sheridan.

"Identical," she replied. "Both were beaten, tied up, then had their fingers cut off, before being left to bleed out from deep cuts in their wrists."

"Right," Jon replied. "So this has to be the same perpetrator, and there has to be some kind of meaning behind the way he kills these girls. He wouldn't do it like that otherwise. Now, Rachel, I believe you have a few more interviews to do with Mollie's student-friends, right?"

"That's right. We'll be there for the morning, I think."

"Okay, now, while there wasn't any obvious link between Mollie and Harper, I also think her friends, Rupa and Bradley, were holding something back. I think Mollie went out to buy some drugs for them to use but got intercepted. I have no idea if that links into her death, but I really want to see if we can push them to admit what Mollie really went out for."

"I can see if I can talk to them again today," Rachel replied.

"That would be good, thanks. So, back to Harper, and the link to the Millers gang. Did we have any developments there?"

"We did, actually," Nathan replied. "It turns out the guy that was with Dillon Harris was Carson Miller."

"He was the one that attacked Tom, right? Seth's flatmate?"

"Right," Nathan replied. "I knew I recognised him from somewhere, but it took some digging last night for me to find the name."

"Is Carson a main member of the family then?"

"Low level, but still a Miller, so yeah."

"I want to talk to him," Jon said.

"Figured you would," Nathan replied with a smile. "I've pulled his details."

"Perfect. What about her missing father, Peter Richards, anything there? Do we even know where he is yet?"

"Nope," Dion replied. "Our Scottish cousins are looking for him, but so far, nothing."

"Damn, he's probably off hunting Nessie or something. Right then, any reports of new bodies, or is our killer having a day off?"

"Nothing yet, guv," Kate replied. Jon nodded. It felt kind of odd her calling him guv after last night, but he'd have to get used to it. He was her boss after all, whether he was just a work colleague or something more. "Looks like our guy might have had a rest."

"Or we just haven't found it yet…" Jon muttered, getting a bad feeling in his gut. This killer wouldn't just stop for no reason.

"Okay," Jon continued. "Rachel, I want you and Nathan at the university finishing off those statements."

"I've got to be at the courthouse again today, but not till later," Nathan cut in.

"Fair enough. Do what you can to help. Meanwhile, Kate and I will see about paying Mr Carson Miller a visit. The rest of you, I'm sure, have lots to be getting on with."

There was a knock on the incident room door. Jon looked up to see Debbie Constable stood outside looking at him.

"Looks like your comment to her yesterday had an effect," Kate commented.

"Mmm," Jon replied and waved for her to come in. "What is it?" he asked as she opened the door.

"We've had a walk-in. Bradley Porter, a friend of Mollie Hayes?"

"Oh, really?"

She nodded. "He's in interview room one."

18

"So, what was Nathan talking to you about?" Kate asked.

"Nothing really," Jon replied as he followed Kate through the station towards the interview suite.

"Really? He was chatting with you for a while."

"Yeah, it was just work stuff," Jon answered, lying through his teeth. He wasn't sure Nathan would appreciate him betraying his trust and outing him.

"Riiight," Kate replied with a suspicious look. "So, it wasn't about me then? He can be a little protective, sometimes."

"I'm sure he just cares about you."

"Yeah. Alright, so, what are you thinking? Why's Bradley here?"

"Guilt," Jon replied, feeling fairly sure about this aspect of the case. "He's not told us something."

"You think it's the drugs angle you were pushing yesterday?"

"Could be," Jon replied. Verbally, he was hedging his bets, but he was secretly about ninety-nine percent sure that was exactly what was happening here, but he didn't want to bet his lunch money on it just yet.

They walked into the interview room to find Bradley sat behind the table. He jumped to his feet as they walked in, pale and nervous.

"Morning, Bradley," Jon began.

"Um, hello."

"It's okay Brad, you can sit," Kate said with a smile, and moved to take her seat. Jon followed, looking over at Bradley, curious to see if his suspicions were right.

"Oh, okay, sorry. Look, I just needed to come and talk to you… again…"

"Brad, wait a moment, yeah?" Kate replied cutting him off, before she then set the DIR to record, and went through the motions of introducing everyone in the room for the benefit of the recording before looking back to Bradley.

"We'll be conducting this interview under Caution Plus Three, Bradley."

"Oh, okay. What's that?"

"I'm going to read you the standard police caution and then I'll explain further," she replied. "In this interview, you do not have to say anything. But it may harm your defence if you do not mention when questioned something which you later rely on in court. Anything you do say may be given in evidence."

"What? So, am I under arrest?"

"No, I'm just telling you what your rights are and the circumstances under which this interview will take place."

Interview, hah! Interrogation, more like, Jon thought.

"Oh..." Bradley replied, frowning.

"Don't worry, it's nothing to be worried about. The Plus Three part of it refers to three things. Firstly, you're not under arrest, secondly, you can leave at any time, and finally, you have the right to free independent legal advice, should you want it."

"It's free?"

"It is."

"Oh, I thought lawyers were really expensive."

"They can be, but this kind of thing is covered."

"Do I need it?"

"Unless you're about to admit to killing Mollie, probably not," Kate replied.

Jon nodded slightly. While Kate's reply wasn't wrong, it was designed to make things move quicker. Getting a lawyer in took time, and always delayed them getting the answers they needed. In fact, time-wasting was a well-known tactic that solicitors used to frustrate the police and protect their clients.

But they needed answers, and quickly, so advising Brad to get some representation would just delay them.

"But it is up to you," Jon added, he didn't want the way they conducted this interview to destroy any future case. "If you feel you need representation, just say so and you can have it. But it will delay things and take time."

"Alright, I don't want to be here any longer than I need to be. I'll continue," Bradley replied.

Jon smiled. "Excellent. Alright, so why did you come to see us today, Bradley?"

"I needed to speak to you. I didn't tell you everything about what Mollie was doing the other night, and I think I need to. I… feel guilty."

"Why? What did you do?"

"Nothing," he replied quickly, and Jon raised an eyebrow in curiosity. "But that's the problem. I should have done something. I should have gone with her. I feel so silly."

"Where did she go?" Jon asked.

"Look, it's nothing serious, okay? We're just having fun. That's all. We don't deal or anything."

"Deal what?" Kate asked. She no doubt knew what Bradley was talking about, but they needed it to come from him, and not to be seen as leading the witness.

Bradley sighed and slumped in his chair, his head low, looking at his hands on the tabletop. "Drugs. She went to buy some weed for us. It should have been my turn to go, but I was just shattered, and I'd done a bunch of the runs recently, covering for Mollie while she finished her work, so I figured that she needed to take her turn. Fair's fair, right?" He sighed again. "I didn't know she'd get killed."

"So," Kate said, cutting in, "you're saying that Mollie, the straight-A student, with an impeccable track record, who everyone loves, was a druggy?"

"No!" Bradley replied, offended. "We were just having a bit of fun, you know? Relaxing and enjoying ourselves. That's all. A bit of weed helped us do that."

"And you let her go out there on her own because you were feeling lazy?"

Bradley frowned and then crossed his arms at Jon's comment. "I think I might need some representation."

"You're doing fine," Kate replied. "I know these are hard questions, but we just need to get to the bottom of all this."

"But, he implied…"

"Just focus on telling us the truth and anything that might help us find out who killed her. That's the most important thing, right?"

"Right. Sure."

"Maybe start with who she was going to see?" Jon said, tilting his head sideways.

"I don't know his real name, but the guy we've been buying the ganja off is called Mogs."

"Mogs?" Kate asked. "M-O-G-S?"

"I think so, I didn't exactly ask him to spell it for me."

"Do you think he did it?" Jon asked.

Bradley shrugged and then shook his head. "Honestly no, probably not. Didn't strike me as that type."

"And, you know that type, do you?"

"What? No! Look, if this is..."

"You did good," Kate cut in. "Is there anything else you can tell us?"

"No, not really. I told you everything else yesterday. I just didn't want to tell you we were buying drugs."

Jon rolled his eyes. He'd felt sure that was the case yesterday, but at least the kid had come forward with it. Kate looked over at him, and Jon nodded to her. They were done here.

"We'll get one of the other officers to come in and formalise a statement and get you home. Thank you for coming in, Bradley. You've been most helpful. But please stay local for a while, will you? No gallivanting off to another part of the country, or going abroad, alright?"

"Sure, no problem," he replied, visibly relaxing now he knew he was off the hook.

A short time later, they were back upstairs in the main office. Jon sat on a chair beside Kate's workstation as she hunted through the database, searching for Mogs.

"You were hard on him," Kate said looking over at him, crossing her legs as she settled into her chair.

Jon bobbed his eyebrows. He was aware he'd been playing bad cop in there and giving Bradley a hard time of it, but honestly, he'd been annoyed and hadn't been feeling charitable. "He messed us about. He should have told us yesterday and not lied."

"I wouldn't say he lied, exactly. He just didn't tell us everything."

Jon grunted. "Yeah, I guess. But that's not much better when people's lives are at risk."

Kate nodded, acknowledging the seriousness of the case and the situation. They needed to work quickly to save any more people from being killed. "Fair point."

"I think that went well, though," Jon remarked. "A bit of good cop, bad cop."

"I'm the carrot and you're the stick, right?"

"You've got the hair for it, carrot top," Jon said, with a wry smile.

Kate turned to him and raised an eyebrow. "Carrot tops are green, smart arse."

"Alright, whatever, Barry. Have we found this Mogs, yet?"

Kate rolled her eyes and returned her attention to the screen, after having logged in and getting to the right program. She popped the name 'Mogs' into the search bar and hit return.

A list of hits popped up, and they started to sift through them, one by one.

"I think this one fits, look," Kate said after a while, pointing to the screen with a slender finger.

Jon gave the profile a look and began to nod. "Freddy 'Mogs' Mogasen," Jon said, reading from his rap sheet. His father was German, his mother English, and he'd been issued warnings, community service, and fines a whole bunch of times, mainly for drugs-related offences, but there was nothing about violent crime on there at all.

"Look," Kate said and pointed using the mouse curser. "Known associates."

"Carson Miller," Jon replied, reading the name. "He certainly gets around. Let's pay him a visit."

19

"Do you think he'll be in?" Kate asked as she drove them towards Cobham village, east of Horsley Station. Carson Miller's address was on their database, so with any luck, it wouldn't be an issue finding him and asking him a few questions.

"I've got no idea. What does the relation of a mob boss do during the day?"

"Beats me," Kate replied. "Manages his racketeering…racket? Maybe?"

Jon laughed. "Yeah, that sounds about right."

"Don't laugh. I've watched *The Godfather*."

"I think you'd be better off watching some of Guy Ritchie's films, to be honest."

"Oh. Makes films about British gangsters, does he?"

"Something like that. There's *Lock, Stock,* and *Snatch*…"

"*Snatch*?"

"Yeah, look it up."

"With a name like that, I'm not sure I want to. Sounds… rude."

"Heh, no. I think you'd like it. It's got Brad Pitt in it."

"Bradders? The Pitt-ster?"

"He's got an Irish accent in it, too."

"Oh, well then, why didn't you say so? He's proper lady-boner material, even now. How old is he now?"

"Lady-boner?"

"Yeah."

"That's a thing?"

"It's totally a thing." She looked over at him with a cheeky smile. "Look it up."

"I'll pass," Jon said and turned to look out the window at the passing houses. They were driving through some wealthy areas with impressive homes. "So, this is how the other half lives, is it?"

"There's a lot of footballers and celebrities around here," Kate said. "Chelsea's training ground isn't far."

"Okay," Jon replied.

"Do you think anything will come from this?"

"Unless we can pin something else on Carson, I doubt it. Tom's already said he doesn't want to press charges," Jon said.

"Yeah, I heard that. They always get away with this shit."

"We still need to talk to him, though. He's linked to all this, and I want to know why. People like him and his family are certainly capable of killing these girls, so just because Tom isn't willing to hold them accountable, doesn't mean we shouldn't."

Kate nodded. "We're getting close."

Jon's phone buzzed in his pocket. He pulled it out and saw the number on the screen, a number he didn't recognise. He nearly hung up, and then thought better of it for some reason, and answered the call.

"Hello?"

"Aaah, Mr Pilgrim. I caught you. Good. I hear you're on your way over to talk to Carson."

Jon frowned at the statement and wondered who the hell this was and how they got his number. "Who is this?"

"My sincerest apologies, where are my manners. My name is Irving Miller. Have you heard of me?"

The jigsaw piece dropped into place, and he wondered how word had gotten out about them making this trip to visit Carson. Who was on the Miller's payroll in the police?

"I have."

"Excellent, Carson is with me, so please come to mine and we can talk about this civilly."

"And where would that be?"

"I'll text you the address," he replied. "See you shortly."

He hung up, and Jon took the phone away from his ear.

"What the hell was that all about?" Kate said, confused.

"Change of plan," Jon said. "That was Irving Miller, we're going to his house to speak to Carson."

"Irving's place? Damn. This just got about a thousand times more serious."

Jon's phone buzzed, announcing the arrival of the text from Irving. He read out the address and Kate popped it into the satnav. It wasn't far.

"Have you dealt with these guys before?" Jon asked feeling slightly nervous.

"No, I've heard about them, but I've not had any dealings with them yet. Not that I'm aware of, anyway. Do you think this is a good idea?"

Jon nodded, although he wasn't totally sure about that. There was every chance that the Millers were luring them into a trap, but somehow, Jon didn't think so. There was nothing to gain from doing that, apart from a whole heap of trouble. "We'll be fine. They won't do anything."

"You think?"

"Pretty positive."

"That's not one hundred percent, though. That's like ninety? Eighty-five? I'm not sure I like the idea of that."

"I get it..."

The rest of the drive didn't take long, and they were soon parking up in the driveway of a gated property. It was a modern, sprawling house... no... mansion was a better term. It was huge and gorgeous.

"You know when they say, crime doesn't pay," Jon said, walking up the driveway beside Kate and gesturing to the house. "Yeah, that's bullshit. It only doesn't pay if you get caught. But if you're good at it, then life's pretty nice."

"I can see that," Kate replied resignedly. "We should plan the perfect crime," she quipped. "I bet that between us, we could come up with something foolproof."

"Foolproof or full proof? Because we'd need to make it proof against more than just fools," Jon remarked.

"Well shit, that counts us out."

"Speak for yourself, Barry."

As they approached the front door, it opened before they reached it, and a man the size of a rhino appeared. He looked them up and down with his beady eyes, before stepping back and waving them in. "Come in," the man of a mountain muttered.

Keeping one eye on the one-man-wrecking ball, Jon walked in first and surveyed the spacious hallway with its immaculate wooden panelling and clean lines. It was a lovely place. Too nice for the likes of gangsters.

"Mr Miller is expecting you," the man rumbled and started across the hall. "Follow me."

Jon looked over at Kate and leaned in to whisper to her, "It speaks."

Kate smirked briefly before getting her face under control as they followed him. His shoulders were so big, Jon could hardly make out the man's head from behind him. It was all neck muscles.

The man ducked through a doorway into one of the rooms and turned to wave them through.

Jon followed and found himself in a large, spacious office. Sofas surrounded a table in the middle of the room and at the far end, a modern desk dominated the far wall. Three people waited for them, all of which Jon recognised from their mug shots and other photos in their files.

Carson sat in a chair before the desk, watching them with a smug expression on his face that Jon wanted to slap right off it again. Irving perched on the front of his desk, sporting a jovial smile, while his wife, Meredith, stood to one side, her look serious and cold.

"Welcome," Irving said in greeting, waving them towards a set of chairs set up before him. "Please, come in. Take a load off. I'm not sure we've ever had the pleasure."

Jon disliked him right away. He was being far too friendly for his own good and decided right away that he was not going to take a seat and get comfortable.

Irving looked at Kate and smiled. "Sergeant Kate O'Connell, I've heard so much about you. Your time on the Surrey Murder Team is well documented. I applaud you. And you..." Irving continued, looking at Jon. "Jon, isn't it? I'm not as familiar with you, Detective Chief Inspector Pilgrim. You're new to the area, right?"

"I am," Jon replied, forcing himself to stay civil. There was no need for this to get out of hand, and judging from the walking lump of muscle behind them, things would go badly for them if it did.

"Laconic. I like it."

"We're here to speak with Carson."

"Right down to business is it? Well, Carson is right here, you can ask him whatever you like."

Jon nodded and was about to say something when Irving cut in again, his tone suddenly serious. "But be aware, Mr Pilgrim, that my family is very dear to me."

"Isn't everyone's?"

Irving paused for a moment. "But of course," Irving replied, his jovial attitude back once more. "Please, go ahead."

"Where were you on the eighth at around three-thirty in the afternoon?"

"At home," Carson replied.

Jon narrowed his eyes at the man. "I have CCTV footage that places you in Sutton."

"You can't believe everything you see on video these days," Carson replied.

"True," Jon answered, nodding his head, "but I think I believe this. Do you know Seth Bailey?"

"Never heard of him," Carson snapped, answering a little too quickly.

"Never?"

"Nope."

"Or, Harper Richards?" Watching closely, he could see the man's face flush with blood as he shifted in his chair at the mention of her name.

"Who's that?" he replied.

"The girl whose murder we're investigating."

"I don't know nothing about no murder."

Jon stared at him for a long moment, deciding if he should pedantically correct his grammar or not. He decided not to, but only just. "So, you've not been watching the news?"

"It's all over the local news, and is even making the national news now," Kate added.

"Of course, we watch the news," Irving cut in. "I think you'll find that what Carson meant is that, while he's aware of recent events, he knows no more than the average person."

"So, why didn't he say that?" Jon asked.

"Because I did," Irving answered, raising his eyebrows. His tone was all serious again, with that hint of threat in his voice.

"Fair enough. Alright, how's business going?"

"Fine," Carson answered.

"You don't work with someone going by the name of Mogs, do you?"

"Um, who?"

"Freddy Mogasen, do you know him?"

"No idea who you're talking about," Carson replied, his smug smile returning.

"I think you're barking up the wrong tree, detective," Irving said.

"You're distressing a member of my family," Meredith added, speaking for the first time. "I think you should leave unless you're going to charge him with anything."

"Well, are you, Detective Pilgrim?" Irving asked.

Jon sighed. "No, not right now."

"Excellent! Then we're done here. I'm pleased this went so well." The man stood and walked up to Jon, putting his arm around his shoulders as he turned him towards the exit. "You know, I wasn't sure how this would go. It's always tricky where new officers are concerned. They don't understand our place in the local community and how valued we are. But, I suppose that will come with time. But please, if you have any further questions, or if you want to work with us on anything, please get in touch. We're huge fans of the police and the work you do for this community."

"I'm sure," Jon replied, speeding up to remove himself from Irving's overly familiar touch. "If we have any further questions, we will be sure to be in touch."

"Of course, anytime. My door's always open."

I bet it is, Jon thought.

In short order, Jon and Kate were back outside and approaching their car. Jon chewed his tongue in frustration, annoyed at how the meeting had gone. They'd got nothing from Carson or Irving, and it felt like they were treating this like a game.

He had little doubt that Irving had some close contacts within the police that he could use to get what he wanted. The fact that the Miller's knew they were coming was enough proof of that.

"Well, that was useless," Jon complained as he settled into the passenger seat.

"I hate dealing with people like that," Kate sympathised. "They always seem to think they're superior. I'd dearly love to take them down a notch or two."

"You and me both," Jon agreed, as he pulled out his buzzing phone, noting it was a call from the office. "Yeah, what's up?"

"Get to Iris Richards' place, she's just called in," Rachel said. "She's been attacked."

"Shit, will do."

"What's going on?" Kate asked as he hung up.

"Harper's mum, she's just been attacked."

20

Kate sped along the main road, their blue lights flashing and the siren baring as they went. Jon helped navigate and worked as a spotter, providing Kate with a second pair of eyes on the surrounding roads.

But she didn't really need him. Her driving was impeccable, and they were soon well on their way towards Epsom, and Iris' house.

"Iris?" Kate asked. "Who'd do that to her? She has nothing to do with this."

"I don't know. I have my suspicions but..."

"The Millers?" Kate suggested.

Jon shook his head. "I doubt it. I can't see them attacking an older woman."

"Is she alright, what did Rachel say?"

"Just that she's been attacked and called it in. I think she's alright."

"I hope so. This is the last thing she needs after losing her daughter."

"No shit," Jon replied as they navigated through the endless roads and into the suburbs of Epsom.

"It could be the Millers," Kate said after a while. "They attacked Tom, although they were going for Seth. What if they thought Seth was hiding out there?"

"Hmm. I wouldn't put it past him. I think Carson knew who we were talking about and was lying through his teeth," Jon said thinking back to the talk they'd just had with the Millers. "He seemed nervous when I brought Harper up. Embarrassed almost, like I'd stumbled onto some kind of huge secret."

"Oh, he knows way more than he's letting on, that's for sure. But we need a little more to go on than just a hunch."

"I know, it's bloody annoying," Jon replied as Kate manoeuvred around traffic that had pulled over for them, and made her way into the estate where Iris lived. As they turned onto her street, Jon spotted the ambulance, a patrol car, and Faith's car parked outside the house.

Kate pulled up and Jon jumped out, rushing up the driveway to knock on the door. Kate joined him moments later.

"Jeez, Pilgrim, I'm in a skirt and heels, slow down."

Jon glanced down, noted the low heels, and raised an eyebrow. "If they're not practical, why'd you wear them?"

Kate shrugged but seemed a little self-conscious, as if he'd pointed something out that he shouldn't. She'd not worn anything like this the first two days, preferring a trouser suit. "Because I wanted to."

"Fair enough. Can't argue with that."

"Good, because I'd bop you on the nose if you did."

Raising his eyebrows in surprise. "You'll bop me?"

"On the schnoz."

"Noted." Jon nodded, and for a moment, hesitated, wondering if he should say what had sprung into his mind. In the end, he chose to throw caution to the wind. "You look nice, though."

"Thank you," Kate replied with a smile, seeming to soak up the compliment.

The door opened. "Hey," Faith said. "You'd better come in"

Jon followed Faith through the hall, past two uniformed officers in the hallway, and into the front room. Iris sat on the sofa beside a paramedic who was tending to her wounds. Another crouched by his bag nearby.

"Hey," Jon said as he walked in. Iris had a developing bruise on her cheek, what would surely be a black eye tomorrow, and a couple of cuts. It also looked like she'd been bleeding from her nose.

"Hi," the crouching paramedic replied without looking up, and handed a fresh wipe to his colleague.

"How is she?"

"She'll survive. No obvious major damage, it all seems superficial. I think we should take her in for some checks, just to be sure but shouldn't be anything to worry about."

"Can she talk?"

"I can talk," Iris replied, brushing the female paramedic's hand away from her face. "It was Seth. He attacked me."

"Seth?" Jon replied. "Are you sure?"

"Of course, I'm sure. I'd know him anywhere. He appeared on my doorstep claiming something or other. I don't know what. Anyway, the next thing I know he's attacking me. Then he ran off."

"You don't know what he wanted?" Jon asked.

"No. He was trying to say something, but I didn't want to listen to him. He's the one that did all this. He killed Harper," she ranted, her voice cracking with emotion until she broke down in tears again.

Jon quietly sighed to himself and turned away while Faith and the paramedics calmed her down and saw to her wounds. Something about this didn't make sense.

Why would Seth come here to attack Iris? What on earth did he think he could gain from it? Was he the killer? Was he trying to take out the whole family? But if that was right, why attack Mollie? Even with the tenuous link through the dealer, Mogs, it just didn't feel right.

"Guv," Kate muttered, her voice low. Jon looked up to see Kate pulling back the curtain on the front window. Behind it, a compact freestanding security camera sat, trained on the area in front of the house.

"Oh," Jon replied and nodded his thanks to Kate before turning back to Iris. "I beg your pardon, but might I ask about the camera in your front window? Is it working?"

"Yeah, helps keep me safe. A fat lot of good it did me today, though."

"May we view the footage from today?"

"My phone. Here, pass it to me." Faith grabbed it and handed it to Iris, who quickly unlocked it and after a few taps, passed it over to Jon before relaxing again.

Jon eyed the screen and the recordings that were on the app as Kate stepped up to him and leaned in to get a closer look.

Tapping on the latest recording, he saw himself and Kate enter the property and tapped back to get to the main screen. After watching Faith and the paramedic's arrival, he finally found what he was looking for.

He didn't rush. He found he enjoyed Kate's closeness as he watched the scene unfold on the small screen. He could feel her warmth and smell her perfume, and for a moment, lost himself in those sensations, imagining getting closer to her.

No, he needed to concentrate.

Jeez, after all his doubts about Kate not having her head in the game, now he was all over the place.

Banishing those, admittedly, pleasant thoughts, Jon focused on the video. He watched as Seth walked up the driveway towards the front door, hesitating a few times, and at one point, actually turning back before he apparently steeled himself and eventually pressed the doorbell.

Iris appeared moments later, yanking open the door, apparently already in a rage. The sound on the video wasn't great, and he kept his volume turned low, but he could make out her frenzied rant easily enough. By contrast, Seth seemed shocked and backed away a step as he tried to talk to her. But his words, whatever they were, just seemed to infuriate Iris even more and she launched herself at him. He tried to fend off her attack, but after a while, his temper clearly got the better of him and he lashed out.

It was one punch, but it caught her right in the face, on her nose and cheek. Iris dropped like a sack of potatoes, twisting as she went so that her face hit the ground.

Seth looked frankly shocked at what he'd done and tried to offer help, but Iris screamed at him and he backed away. Eventually, as it became clear she would have nothing to do with him, he walked off, leaving her as she continued to shout and pulled out her phone saying she'd report him.

Jon looked up at Kate as the video ended and her expression mirrored his own thoughts.

Seth had hardly attacked her. He was defending himself if anything. That didn't excuse punching her, but it was hardly the premeditated attack that Iris was making out to be.

"I'm going to need this video," Jon said. "If that's ok?"

"Of course, you can take it. I think there's an option to email the videos to wherever," Iris said dismissively. Jon nodded to Kate and handed her the phone. She took it and went to work.

"Iris, can I talk to you about what I just watched?"

"What of it?"

"You attacked him, Iris. He only defended himself and lashed out in a temper. You're lucky he didn't fight back, frankly."

"No, he assaulted me. He broke my nose."

"I don't think it's broken," the paramedic cut in.

"I know these kinds of confrontations can seem scary and intense, Mrs Richards, but if you watch that video, I think you'll find that what I'm saying is true."

"Whatever. I know he killed my baby. I know it. What I did to him is nothing compared to what he did to Harper."

"And if he didn't kill her?"

"No, he did. I know it. He deserved everything he got today. Everything. Now give me back my phone. Now!"

Kate did as she asked but then nodded to Jon, signalling that she'd emailed the video. Iris threw the phone down beside her and sat back. "My nose hurts."

With a sigh, Jon turned away. He had to remember that she was under an awful lot of stress right now and probably wasn't thinking straight. Even if Seth did want to report her, Jon doubted that anything would come of it, partly because he hit her back.

Jon's phone buzzed in his pocket.

Fishing it out, he noted the display proclaiming that it was a call from Horsley Station.

"Go," he said as he answered.

"We've got another body," Rachel said.

"Another one?" Jon replied as he walked outside, Kate on his heels.

"Yeah. Same MO, but this one's a bit strange."

"Strange?"

"It's um… well, best you go and have a look yourself, I think. I've only had a brief description, and I don't think I read it right."

"Send me the address," he replied. "We're on our way."

21

"She said it was the same MO?" Kate asked.

Jon nodded. "That's what she said. I'm guessing we have the same missing fingers and cuts, but she said it was strange, too."

"Strange?"

"Yeah. No idea what she means by that."

"Feck, this just keeps getting worse. I'm not sure what's going on anymore."

Jon sighed. "I know what you mean. It's a mess."

"Good, because that video of Seth, it looked like he'd come to talk to her, not to fight, or attack her. He looked scared."

"I'd be scared of Iris if she came at me," Jon replied. "She's a formidable woman. But yeah, you're right. I honestly don't think Seth killed Harper. His relationship with her might be troubled, but... murder? I just don't know."

"No, me neither. It just doesn't ring true. I think the Miller angle is more fertile. Maybe one of them, Carson perhaps, has taken a liking to killing young women and thought Harper was a good first choice."

"Mollie was a pretty girl, too," Jon mused, making links in his mind. "Maybe Carson saw her buying from Mogs and she caught his eye."

Kate nodded. "I think that's a better angle than Seth. I can see Carson doing something like that, with that smug grin on his face as he watches them bleed out."

"I wanted to wipe that smile from his face the moment I walked in there," Jon admitted, remembering the cruel, self-entitled smile that was on the little shit's face the entire time they were there.

"I'd have been next in line," Kate replied, her voice full of venom. "So, what do we do?"

"We need more evidence. We need something to hang our hat on. If we arrest Carson now, without a shred of evidence, we could be up shit creek without the proverbial."

Kate drove into the outskirts of Reigate and navigated through the streets until they reached the residential road, lined with rows of three-storey, redbrick terrace houses. Part of the road had been cordoned off with blue and white police tape and there was no way they were going to get closer. Jon noted the presence of a few media vans and grumbled to himself. "Shit, I thought we were getting lucky with this case. I hoped they were preoccupied with the Devlin thing. But it looks like the press got wind of it anyway."

"They always do," Kate remarked.

"Yeah, no shit. Come on, let's get in there."

Parking up, Jon got out and walked with Kate towards the house. As they got close, a blond-haired man broke away from the gathered onlookers and approached them.

"DC O'Connell?" the man called out.

"Not now, Chester," Kate replied, raising her hand to him.

"Is this another murder? Do we have a serial killer on our hands?"

Kate stopped, sighed, and looked up at him. "Firstly, it's DS O'Connell, Chester. You know that. And second, no comment."

"Still no Nathan, I see. Have you two fallen out?"

With a grunt, Jon stepped forward and ushered the man out of the way as they approached the line.

"It's DCI Pilgrim, right?" Chester said, undeterred. "Jon Pilgrim? From Nottingham Police? You're a long way from your patch, Jon. A long way from Charlotte."

Jon froze. He spun on Chester as heat and fire inside bubbled up. The reporter raised his hands in a gesture of surrender and took a step back.

"Never say her name, again," Jon grunted, his tone low as he pointed a finger at Chester. The reporter shrugged but said nothing.

Jon reigned in his fury as Kate appeared beside him.

"Leave him, he's not worth it," she said, guiding him away. "Come on."

Jon nodded and moved to the nearby officer who let them through the cordon and away from the press.

"Sorry," Jon said. "I just..."

"It's okay," she said. "You don't need to say anything if you don't want to."

"No, I do, but..." He sighed. "You should know, especially if we're going to be working together going forward. Later maybe."

Kate nodded. "Sound good."

"Right, come on, let's go and see what we have in here," Jon said. They moved to a nearby van and pulled on forensic suits before they set off towards the front of the house. Turning in and making for the front door, Damon stepped out and did a double-take as he spotted Jon.

"Pilgrim, wait, just stop right there."

Jon paused and looked at him quizzically. "Sure, what's up?"

"You don't want to go in there."

"Why?" Jon asked raising an eyebrow.

"Trust me, you really don't."

"I'm not sure I follow. We need to see the crime scene."

"I get that, but in this case, I think you should sit this one out and let Kate go up alone."

"What? No! Unless you tell me what the hell you're talking about, I'm heading straight in there."

Damon looked torn and after a moment's thought, sighed and looked back at him. "He's mimicked the Doll Killer," Damon replied. "He's mimicked Charlotte's murder."

"What!" Jon said, raising his voice as a chill raced up his spine.

Damon raised his hands as Jon took a step towards him. "Please, I don't think you should go in there. I really don't."

Stepping up to Damon, Jon pushed past him as a deep need to get up there filled him. "I need to see this," he said and strode into the house and up the stairs. Following the trail of the attending SOCOs into the front bedroom, he was greeted with a nightmare from his past.

As he took in the scene he felt the blood drain from him, leaving him dizzy and light-headed. In that instant, he was back in his house in Nottingham five years ago looking at Charlotte.

In the centre of an otherwise bare spare room, the woman was strung up in a standing position. Handcuffs were on her wrists, pulling her arms out wide. Metal wire attached the cuffs to sturdy bolts drilled into the joists above the ceiling, holding the young woman up in an almost Christ-like pose. One of her legs hung loosely to the floor, her toes just brushing the carpet. A third set of cuffs and a wire had been attached to her left ankle, holding it up and bending her leg like a ballerina.

He'd dressed her up, too.

It was just like the Doll Killer, she had the tutu on as well. Everything was there.

Images of Charlotte flashed through his mind. He remembered finding her strung up, dead eyes staring at nothing, the horrific painted face the killer had given her.

Jon moved around to her front which faced the far window that looked out onto the street. Sure enough, her face was painted white, with bright red lips, red circles on her cheeks, and a red line that had been painted vertically above and below her eyes like a clown. The woman's head hung limply, her strong red hair falling about her face.

"Holy shit," Kate gasped as she entered the room.

Staring at the corpse, Jon could only see Charlotte. It was her, just as he remembered. It was happening again. The nightmare was back and all too real. He wished he could have saved her from this madman, and they could have lived together, maybe got married and had a family. He missed her so much. Reaching out, he went to touch her face one last time.

"Jon!" Kate called out.

He snapped out of it and Charlotte's face was gone. Feeling weak, Jon stumbled back towards the wall, unable to pull his eyes away from the nightmare before him. Kate was instantly beside him, catching him.

"Hey, it's okay. Come on, let's get you out of here."

He let her guide him, her arm around his body as she walked him out onto the landing. There was a small bench beside the bannister where she sat him down. As he sat, the emotion of the moment suddenly caught up with him and he felt tears sting his eyes.

He pressed the palms of his hands into his eyes and rubbed them. "Shit."

"It's okay," Kate said, sat beside him.

"No, it's not. It's not okay. He knows. Somehow, this guy, he knows."

"Knows what?"

"About my girlfriend, about what happened to her. How does he know? Fuck. I'm sorry. I'm a mess."

"It's fine. I get it. I do."

"I need to tell you…"

"You can, but later. We'll get a drink tonight. We can talk then, okay?"

"Yeah, sounds good," he replied, relieved that he'd be able to talk it through with her. He'd been thinking that he'd need to tell her about it, and this would be that chance. Looking up, he met her gaze and smiled. "Thank you."

"It's okay. Now, do you think you can hold it together and go back in there?"

Honestly, he wasn't a hundred percent sure, but he'd try. He needed to do this. People were relying on him.

"How is he?" Jon looked up to see his old friend looking down at them. He felt grateful he was here.

"He's fine," she replied.

"I'm okay, Damon. Seriously. It was just a shock," Jon reassured him.

"If you need time, or need to step away from this..."

"No. No way. I want to see this through," he said standing up. "I need to find this bastard."

Damon nodded. "Alright then, but seriously, no one would think less of you if you couldn't."

"I know, but I need to do this. I need to face the memories," he replied and steeled himself with a deep breath before walking back into the room. This time, he pushed the thoughts of Charlotte back into the deepest parts of his mind and did his best to view the scene as a detective.

"This is messed up," Kate said as Jon slowly circled the corpse. Looking up, he noted the girl's right hand. The same two fingers were missing again, severed from just below the knuckle with a ragged cut. Jon grimaced at the now-familiar calling card that this killer left. He spotted the long cuts that had been made along the length of her forearms. He noted the dried blood that had run down her arms and body, before pooling on the floor beneath her.

"This is a message for me," Jon said.

"For us," Damon added.

"You've seen people killed like this before?" Kate asked.

"Not exactly the same," Damon replied. "My last big case with Jon in the Nottingham Police was someone the press called the Doll Killer. He killed women, usually by strangulation, then washed them, dressed them, painted their faces, and strung them up. They all looked like this, like marionettes. It was the strangest thing I'd ever seen at the time. And the last victim, the final victim, was Charlotte—Jon's girlfriend."

"I'm so sorry," Kate said.

Jon nodded, preferring not to think about it too much. It was a long time ago, even though it often felt like only yesterday.

"Right, okay, so this Doll Killer, I'm guessing he didn't cut fingers off, right?"

"No, he didn't," Jon replied. "He didn't slash wrists either."

"*This* guy though, he's done his research. He clearly knows your history," Damon said.

"No shit."

"I've worked some cases in my time," Sheridan said as she walked into the room. "But this one is something else."

"Hey," Kate said in greeting.

"Afternoon," Jon said and pointed to the corpse. "Same but different, right?"

"Right," Sheridan replied. "It's the same killer, I'm sure of it. I know he's dressed the scene up differently, but the details are the same. Same missing fingers, same method."

"Who's the girl? Kate asked.

"Emily Murphy," Sheridan replied.

"What?" Jon said. "Fucking hell, really?"

"What?" Sheridan replied.

Damon hung his head and put his hands on his hips. "Of course."

"Is someone going to explain?" Kate said.

"My girlfriend's name was Charlotte Murphy," Jon said, shaking his head. He turned away and kicked the wall gently.

"Oh," Kate replied.

"Her boyfriend, Morgan, is downstairs if you want to talk to him," Sheridan said.

"I think we'll have someone else take that statement," Kate suggested.

Jon looked up at her and smiled, grateful that she was looking out for him. He wanted to find the killer, but talking to the boyfriend was not something he felt in any mood to do. In fact, right now, he just wanted to step away for a few hours and come back to it fresh tomorrow.

Turning, Jon looked through the window to the street beyond. The evening was drawing in and the lights from the police vehicles were casting a blue and red glow across the houses opposite. Taking in the view, Jon emptied his mind of the horror that was behind him and closed his eyes. He couldn't let this killer get into his head. He needed to be stronger than him. He needed to see this through, find this sicko, and end this.

But not tonight. Tonight he needed some time. He needed to step away and get some distance from it all.

Kate stepped up beside him. "How're you feeling?"

"Tired," Jon replied.

"Do you still want to get that drink?"

"Is it still on offer?"

"Of course."

"Then, yes. The sooner, the better."

"How about now?"

22

"We don't have to talk if you don't want to," Kate said. "We can just sit here in silence, knowing you're with a friend. I don't mind."

They sat in the back of the pub on a sofa, their drinks on the table beside them.

Jon nodded as he thought back to that room and the poor girl who'd become the latest victim of this killer. A killer who clearly knew who was after him, and was letting them know he knew. The killer was taunting them, showing them how powerful he was, how superior he felt compared to them, and so far, he was right. They had no solid leads and seemed no closer to finding him than they had been three days ago.

It was all so frustrating, and it was not helped by his current state of mind. Everything was all tangled up in a chaotic mess up there. He couldn't make much sense of anything, he needed to offload some of his baggage. He needed to talk.

"I want to talk about it," Jon said. "I need to. I think I owe you that much."

"You don't owe me anything," Kate replied.

"Thanks, but I have to do this, for my own sake as much as anyone else's."

"It's up to you. I'm happy to listen if it helps."

"Thanks," Jon replied with a weak smile.

Kate leaned in and put her hand on his. "Anytime."

Jon nodded. "Damon was right. We'd been hunting this guy—Jimmy Sutton was his name—he'd been killing young women and turning them into marionettes, just like today's victim. The press dubbed him the Doll Killer, because of course they would. They have to have their cute names."

"Always," Kate agreed.

"He'd kill them, wash them, and then paint their faces like dolls. Then he'd dress them in tutus and dancer's outfits with tall socks and stuff. Put their hair in bunches or pigtails. It was a whole routine for him. And once he was done, he'd string them up, posing them like dancers or dolls. It was the strangest case. In the end, he pleaded insanity, saying a doll in his house had told him to do it."

"Wow," Kate replied. "That's messed up."

"I know. We never found the doll he ranted about while in custody either."

"So, how did he end up focusing on you?"

"I'd been on TV. We were running low on leads and needed to re-energise the case. So the victims' families clubbed together and put a reward out that would go to anyone who gave information that would directly lead to the killer's arrest. That's when Sutton called me. He taunted me.

So I turned it around on him and put the recording of his voice out on the news."

"Clever."

"I thought so. Anyway, Sutton's mother heard it and recognised him. She confronted him, but he turned violent. She managed to barricade herself in the bathroom and call us, naming him and giving us his address before he got through the door. He killed her too, but we had him then. We knew who he was, but he also knew we were closing in on him. That's when he turned his attention to me. He tracked me down and attacked Charlotte while I was at work. We caught him later that day, only for me to return home and find her. I'll never forget what she looked like. Ever."

Kate grabbed his hand and held it in hers. "I'm so sorry."

"It's okay."

"You must miss her."

He nodded. "Every day. I sometimes think about what could have been if things had turned out differently. But she's gone, I've done my grieving. I miss her, but I couldn't wallow in that grief. That's not me."

"I understand."

"It's not something that normally bothers me or takes up much mental space, apart from the occasional nightmare, but seeing that today was just too much."

"I understand. If there's anything I can do…"

"Thanks for listening to me," Jon replied with a smile. "I really appreciate it."

"Of course," she replied.

She looked sad, Jon thought, and her eyes seemed to drift into the middle distance. "It kind of reminds me of what happened to me," she said.

Jon nodded. "Devlin, right?"

She nodded.

"Your neighbour lived though."

"Oh, yeah, but that's not what I'm talking about. My history with Devlin goes back even further than that."

"Aaah?" Jon replied, and remembering what Nathan had said, that there was more to this Devlin thing than he was aware of.

"When I was sixteen, my Aunt Fiona was killed in Ireland, near Cork. Devlin did it. He took her to a stone circle in the countryside and killed her on the central plinth. Fiona and I were close, and being a stupid teenager I went looking for the killer because the Garda couldn't track him down. I failed too, but while I was there, unknown to me at the time, I met Devlin when I visited the crime scene. Afterwards, he started sending me letters. At least one a year, taunting me and threatening me."

"Shit, I had no idea."

"Fiona's death was why I joined the police. I wanted to find her killer. That, and my dad was in the Royal Ulster Constabulary."

Jon nodded with a smile. "My dad was a uniformed officer too. Seems like we have that in common as well."

Kate chuckled. "Yeah. So, cut to ten years later, I join the Murder Team as a detective. Nathan and I hunt down Wilson Hollins. The guy I told you about who killed his former school bully."

"I remember, the guy who was sacrificed, right?"

"That's the one. Our second big case was a guy called Solomon Lichwood. He was a photographer who kidnapped four models. He killed them in several derelict buildings in the county and took photos of them. The third case was Terry Sims, who was hunting that book I mentioned."

"The one who was working for Abban, right?"

"That's right. The thing was, all three cases were linked. There was, and maybe still is, a group of wealthy, corrupt men who organised all these killings, They got Wilson and Solomon to make sacrifices for their group."

"So, they're like a cult?"

"I think so. Abban was one of the wealthy guys. I don't know what happened to the group, but they've been quiet for a while now. Maybe they're gone for good, but I somehow doubt it."

"Sounds like you've had it bad," Jon said.

Kate smiled. "Yeah, I guess. I think we've both had some messed up shit happen to us."

Jon nodded, feeling a strong sense of empathy towards her. She'd suffered at the hands of a determined psychopath and had a prolonged reign of terror perpetrated against her for years, and yet, here she was, still fighting, still working to stop the bad guys.

"You've done amazingly well, given the circumstances. Seriously. I'm beyond impressed. Not many could do what you've done."

"You're still here, too. Still fighting."

"Yeah," he replied. "Charlotte's death changed me, for sure. I knew what I had to do after that. I have to stop them. I have to hunt down these vicious killers and bring them to justice. It's been my mission in life from that day to this."

"A worthy fight, if ever there was one," Kate said with a smile, squeezing his hand.

Jon smiled back and nodded, looking down at their interlocked hands. He enjoyed the warmth and softness and appreciated her care and attention. She knew what he'd been through, and could sympathise because she'd been through something similar.

He felt a connection that he'd not felt with anyone else since Charlotte. It was something he never thought he'd feel again and found it comforting. It was an amazing feeling of relief, warmth, and friendship... and maybe something more.

He wasn't sure of that, but he hoped he'd found a good friend at the very least.

Without warning, Kate placed her hand on the side of his face as she leaned in. She lifted his head and kissed him on the lips. Shocked, Jon sat rooted to the spot for the few seconds that it lasted, enjoying it, but also not entirely sure if he wasn't just imagining things. It seemed to come out of nowhere, and yet, somehow it felt right.

She pulled away, looked him in the eye, and then glanced away. "Um, I'm sorry. I don't know... I didn't mean..."

"No, it's fine, it's..." he smiled at her and found her gaze again. A feeling of relief washed over him. He knew that at some level she must feel something like what he was feeling towards her. "It's amazing, in fact."

"You're sure?" she asked, hesitant.

"Positive," he replied, and this time, he kissed her.

23

Abban sat on the hard bench in the back of the van as it rattled along the road, bouncing over potholes and generally causing him a great deal of discomfort.

These last few weeks of the trial had been one humiliation after another as his life had been laid bare for all the world to see, and it wasn't over yet. He still had the case in Ireland to look forward to, which no doubt would be just as bad.

Terry had played his part, taking the heat for many of the crimes that had been committed, but this Irish case might be different. He didn't have a scapegoat in place this time, and he wondered how that might impact his chances.

Still, he was a wealthy man, and he would be sure to enlist the best solicitor that money could buy to represent him.

"Comfortable?" the officer in the back said to him with a sneer. It had not escaped Abban's notice that he was sat on a cushion.

"Endlessly," Abban replied, wishing he could knock that grin off the other man's face.

Tyres screeched outside. The van swerved violently, then something hit it. Abban was thrown from the bench and slammed to the floor, his cuffed hands doing little to save him.

The vehicle tipped and landed on its side. Metal screeched, deafening in the enclosed space. A second later, it came to a rest and Abban slowly sat up.

He dare not believe what this might mean as he found his feet. At his feet, the uniformed officer lay on what had been the side of the van, his nose bleeding as his eyes wheeled around in confusion.

"What the…?" the officer said.

Seconds later, he heard scuffles and shouts, followed by a thud. Then the sound of a chain being dragged over concrete, followed by a clang at the door. Abban watched closely, wondering what was happening. An engine revved, and a beat later, the van lurched before the rear door was yanked off its hinges.

The door clattered to the tarmac ten metres away on the end of a chain that had been attached to the tow bar at the back of a white van a short distance away.

Abban smiled and looked down at the officer on the floor.

"Night night," he said, and kicked him in the face several times, getting a great sense of enjoyment out of it.

The officer stopped moving, and Abban paused to catch his breath before looking up at the figure that stood outside, waiting for him.

24

A loud, incessant noise rang through the room and right into the deepest recesses of Jon's mind. The irritating buzz startled him and brought him to instant wakefulness. Looking up, he gazed across the unfamiliar room and blinked.

"What the hell?" he muttered, and then noticed the glow from a phone on the desk halfway across the room.

Beside him, a warm body shifted, her hand reaching across his bare chest as she grumbled. "Ignore it, it'll go away."

He looked down to see Kate snuggled up beside him, her eyes closed and her auburn hair loose instead of in her usual ponytail.

Shit. Remembering the night before, he couldn't quite believe where he was or what had happened, and yet, here she was, in bed, and pressed up against him.

The buzzing phone continued to sound through the room, loud and insistent.

"Ugh," Kate groaned. "Really?"

"You could just ignore it," Jon offered.

BUUUUZZZZZ!

"No, no, I'd better get it," she replied jumping out of bed. Jon watched her move as the filtered light from a streetlamp outside caught her pale skin. He couldn't help but stare in wonderment at her and the frankly bizarre situation he found himself in.

He felt like an eighteen-year-old again after his first time being with a girl and waking up in her bed.

Wrapping her arms around her bare chest, she looked back at him as she stumbled over the discarded clothes on the floor and flushed. She waved her hand at him. "Stop looking."

"I like looking," he replied with a smile.

She rolled her eyes, picked up her phone, and answered.

"Hello?"

"DC O'Connell?" In the silence of the room, he could hear the male voice on the other end of the line easily.

"Yeah… I mean, yes?"

"Ma'am, it's Officer Davis from Mount Browne. Apologies for the early wake-up call, but we need you to come in." He'd not been to the Surrey Police Headquarters known as Mount Browne in Guildford, but he'd heard of it.

"Oh?" she replied frowning back at Jon.

"Sorry, I know it's early," Officer Davis continued. "But there's been a development in the Devlin case, and we need you to come in right away. It's urgent. How fast can you get to us?"

"Um," Kate looked over at him and pulled a face. "Pretty quick, I guess. What's happened?"

"I'm afraid I'm not at liberty to say, we just need you to come in, ASAP."

"Alright, yeah, sure. I'll be on the road in five."

"Excellent, I'll meet you in reception."

"Okay, thanks."

Kate clicked off the call. "Well, that sucks."

"Duty calls?"

"Yeah, something about the Devlin case. No idea what. I'd better get going though." Flipping on a light, Kate hopped over to the nearby chest of drawers and rummaged through it. Jon watched her rush about her studio flat naked, picking up clothes and cursing up a storm. He just sat back, enjoying the view.

"Damn it… Where is that… Ah, got it. Right," she said. Clutching the bundle of clothing to her chest, she walked over to him and perched on the side of the bed. "I'm sorry."

"It's okay, that's the life of a police officer. Do you want me to—?" He pointed towards the front door, indicating that she might want him to leave.

"No," she cut in. "You stay there. Get up when you're ready, there's no rush. If you can find some breakfast in the kitchen, you're welcome to it. I'll see you at the station later, okay?"

"Okay."

"This isn't how I planned this morning to go."

"It's okay, and thank you for last night."

She raised an eyebrow.

"No. Not that. Although, that was fun too. No, I mean for listening to me, I really appreciate it. I needed that."

"My pleasure." She smiled. "Be back in a moment," she said, getting up to run towards her bathroom before turning back and leaning in to give him a quick kiss. Seconds later, she disappeared into the bathroom.

Jon laid back, putting his hands behind his head, and took a deep breath as he thought back over the previous evening, and smiled.

This didn't feel like some meaningless encounter, it felt better than that. It felt deeper and stronger. It felt right, somehow.

Moments later, Kate reappeared, buttoning her shirt, wearing her usual trouser suit.

"It's a nice place you have here," Jon remarked, looking around.

"Thanks. It's alright, I suppose. It could do with some work though."

"Really?"

"Yeah. A new lick of paint would be good, plus some other bits. Which reminds me, I need to talk to Francine downstairs."

"Does some DIY on the side, does she?" Jon asked.

Kate snorted. "No, she's an old woman. She's had a handyman in recently doing some jobs for her. I see their van out front all the time but I keep forgetting to ask her for their number." She dashed into the kitchen and grabbed a cereal bar which she tore into with gusto before hunting for her shoes.

"Well, if you do, and they're good, keep hold of it in case I need them once I get my own place."

"Will do," she mumbled around a mouthful of cereal bar.

Finding her shoes after a brief hunt, Kate sat on the edge of the bed and pulled them on.

"Will you be okay?" she asked.

"I'm fine. Go on, don't want to upset the top brass."

"The door is on the latch, so just close it when you leave."

"Will do," he replied.

Kate winked and smiled. "See you later," she said, and within seconds she was out of the flat, her footsteps fading down the corridor and then down the stairs to the ground floor. He heard the building's front door go, and then moments later a car start up and pulled away.

Jon sat up in Kate's bed, leaning against the headboard as he looked around the modest living space. The main room incorporated her bed, living room, and kitchen, with only her bathroom behind another door. Despite its size, it was clean and tidy, and actually really nice. Only Jon's discarded clothing on the floor marred its appearance.

Feeling wide awake, he figured he might as well get up rather than try to sleep anymore. He could even head back to his hotel room for a change of clothes before heading in. If he got a move on, he might even miss the traffic.

Jumping out of bed, Jon quickly got dressed and used the bathroom. While he was in there, he squidged some of Kate's toothpaste onto his finger and rubbed it on his teeth, before heading to the kitchen and getting himself a glass of water.

After a brief hunt, he found some bread and slipped a slice into the toaster before looking for the margarine. Two minutes later he was munching through a warm slice of buttery toast and admiring the photos on Kate's shelves. As he looked over the images of Kate and her family, full of life and smiles, something about them began to nag at the corner of his thoughts, but he couldn't quite put his finger on what it was.

As he looked from one photo to another, his phone rang.

"Hello?"

"Pilgrim, it's Nathan."

"Jesus, you're in early."

"Haven't you heard? I practically live here."

"No one told me they provided bed and breakfast. Is the rent cheap? I'm looking for a place."

"Oh, it's cheap, just bloody uncomfortable. Look, where are you?"

Jon hesitated as he looked around the room and decided to lie. "At my place, why?"

"We've had another walk-in, can you get into the station quickly?"

"Yeah, sure. Who is it?" Jon's eyebrows rose as Nathan told him. "I'll be right in."

25

As Jon walked into the office, darkness blanketed the Surrey countryside outside the station's windows, and the SIU remained quiet, with only a few lights on. Nearby, Nathan sat before a single illuminated desk. Further back, members of the night shift were finishing off their work.

Walking into his private office, Jon threw his things into it before walking over to Nathan.

"Morning, Fox."

"Pilgrim," Nathan replied. "Sorry to call you in so early, but I didn't think this could wait."

"No, you did right. So, what happened?"

"Seth just turned up in reception a couple of hours ago," Nathan replied. "Said he wanted to talk to you and set things right. He's been with his solicitor since then, but I think they're ready for you now."

"Okay, great. This is unexpected, but I'll take it," Jon replied.

"So, I've been calling Kate, but…"

"Oh, yeah. She was called into Mount Browne early, something to do with the Devlin extradition."

"Oh," Nathan replied with a frown and then shrugged. "Fair enough."

"So, where is he?"

"Interview room three," Nathan replied. "Do you need a second in there with you?"

"No, you're good. I'll go on my own."

"Alright, see you in a bit," Nathan replied, and returned to his work as Jon walked back to his office and picked up his files. In less than five minutes, he was walking into the interview room where Seth and his lawyer waited.

Thin and tall, Seth had a wiry strength to him and a gaunt look to this face. He didn't look healthy.

"Good morning, Mr Bailey," Jon said.

"Y'alright?" Seth replied.

Jon nodded as he dropped his files on to the table and nodded to the solicitor sat beside him. "I'm DCI Jon Pilgrim."

"Ana Allen, of Marshall and Edwards Solicitors, Guildford," she replied with a brief, professional smile.

"Nice to meet you, Ana," he said. She was all business with her scraped back hair and prim suit.

"And you. Shall we start?"

Jon nodded and started the PIR before running through the usual introductions for the benefit of the recording.

"So, Seth. You came to us, so would you like to tell me why you're here? What led you to come in today?"

He nodded and sat forward. "I just needed to set things straight. It wasn't right that I was out there, hiding when I knew Harper was dead. I just... I couldn't do it any longer. I needed to come and set the record straight. Especially after that whole Iris thing yesterday." He did seem exhausted.

"You mean the attack?"

"I didn't attack her!"

"I didn't say that," Jon replied, keeping his voice calm and even.

"Oh, well, yeah. But she did. She said it right to my face. She's crazy!"

Jon pulled a face. "She's a grieving mother who just lost her only daughter in a violent murder. So, I think it's fair to say that her judgement might be a little impaired. I think we can cut her a little slack."

"She thinks I did it, though."

"Are you saying you didn't?"

"No. I'd never do that," Seth protested. "I couldn't."

"So, why don't you tell me what did happen? That is why you're here, right?"

Seth sighed and nodded. "It is."

"In your own time," Jon said after a moment of silence. He didn't want to be sat here for too long.

"Harper and I, we argue sometimes. We've always been a bit like that, but this was different. I messed up, and I wish I could take it back, but I can't. I fucked up, and now she's dead."

"How did you mess up?" Jon asked as he made notes.

Seth sighed again, and there seemed to be some kind of internal struggle going on, like he wanted to talk, but part of him was resisting too. But after a moment, his honest side won out. "I cheated on her. I had a one-night stand and… and she found out."

"Ah. So, that was the argument you had?"

"Yeah. Well, kinda."

"Kinda?"

"She found out like, a week before that, and a few days later, she did the same thing back. She cheated on me for revenge. Can you believe that? I mean, what kind of b…" He bit his tongue, stopping himself from saying something he might regret. "It's just, that's messed up."

"I see," Jon replied.

"But that's not all. She slept with Carson Miller! Fucking Miller! I can't believe she'd do that to me, and I think she told him too. I mean, talk about psycho."

"So that's what you were fighting over?"

"Yeah! She did it on purpose. She knows the Millers hate me."

"And why do they hate you, Seth?" Jon asked.

Ana leant in. "You don't have to answer anything you don't want to," she warned him.

"I know. I know what I'm doing," he replied with a sigh. "They don't like me because of some of my friends. They... I know some people in the Kings Gang, that's all."

"You know some people?"

"Just some friends. That's not illegal, is it?"

"No," Jon replied, a little surprised with his honesty. Although he felt sure that Seth's association with the Kings was perhaps a little stronger than that. "Do you deal drugs for them?"

Seth clamped his mouth shut and stared at Jon.

"We know you've dealt drugs in the past," Jon continued. "Also, given that the Millers came looking for you, I think there's more to it than you just knowing some people in a rival gang."

Seth seemed nervous, and looked around, apparently searching for the right answer on the walls or floor somewhere.

Jon needed more from Seth. "You want to do the right thing for Harper, right? You want to clear your name and help us find the man who killed her?"

"Yeah," Seth replied, looking tired.

"Then you need to tell me what the hell's going on."

"Alright, yeah, I did some deals with them a while back. Moved some of their drugs, that kind of thing... and I might have moved on some of the Miller's territory. I don't do as much now, but they hate me, Carson and the Millers."

"So, as far as Carson sees it, you're a member of a rival gang?"

Seth nodded. "I'm not, but yeah, that's right. I knew I had to leg it when she told me what she'd done. I knew they'd come looking for me. That Carson, he'd take it as a personal insult. I didn't know Harper was dead until a day or so ago. I had no idea. I knew she went to her mum's, but I didn't know…" Seth buried his head in his hands and grunted. "He did it, didn't he? Carson did it. He killed her."

"I can't comment on that, Mr Bailey. But, seems you were right about Carson taking things personally, because he went to your flat and assaulted your flatmate, Tom Poole."

"Shit. Is he alright?"

"The last I heard, he's in the hospital. They did some serious damage to him."

"Fuck. I told him to leave, the bloody idiot. Why didn't he listen?"

"I don't think he believed you. He'll survive, no thanks to you."

Seth grumbled.

"Right, so let's get this straight," Jon said looking at his notes. "You cheated on Harper and she found out, so she then cheated on you with a Miller, knowing it would cause you problems when they found out who she was and who she'd been dating, which they clearly did."

"Yeah, that's about it."

"How did they find out? You said you think she told Carson."

"Yeah, maybe. I don't know."

"Right. So, I take it you were angry at Harper, right?"

"Yeah," Seth replied, just as Ana went to advise him. She then pulled a face and rolled her eyes. "I was pissed, but I wouldn't kill her."

"How do I know that, Mr Bailey? How do I know you wouldn't get so angry that you might take things a step too far?"

"Piss off. I'd never do that. I couldn't"

"How do we know?"

Seth blinked for a moment.

"Because of where you told me you were that night," Ana reminded him.

"Oh, yeah. I have an alibi," Seth replied. "I went to Tiana's place."

"Who's Tiana?" Jon asked, feeling exasperated.

"The, uh… The girl… The one I… you know, went with."

"You went back to the girl you slept with?"

Seth flushed. "Yeah. I know how that sounds."

"You're not kidding. So, she'll back you up on this, under oath if need be?"

"I think so."

"Right, well we're going to need to speak with her."

"I know," Seth replied. "I'm not proud of what I did, but Harper did just as bad. I didn't want her to die, though. This is all so messed up. I couldn't hide forever, and I want you guys to find the pissant that did this, that's why I came in."

"That's admirable," Jon replied. "Providing your story checks out."

Seth nodded, only for the door behind Jon to burst open. He turned to see Nathan stood there, flustered, a look of terror on his face. He waved vigorously at Jon. "You need to come with me right now."

Jon frowned. "Uh, okay. Right, thank you, Seth. Stay here, we'll need to ask you some more questions I think. Bear with me."

Leaving the room, Jon walked up the corridor to Nathan, who stood shifting from foot to foot.

"What is it?" Jon asked.

"So, I was thinking, what you said about Kate being called in early, it didn't feel right, but I couldn't think why until I checked my news feed." Nathan held up his phone to show a headline.

Kidnapper escaped. Abban Devlin has escaped from police custody while being extradited from the UK to Ireland.

"What?" Jon asked as a deep-seated fear started to take root in his gut and tie it in knots. "He's free?"

"Looks that way. When I saw that, I knew something was wrong, so I called Mount Browne. They have no record of anyone calling Kate. Plus, she's not been signed into Mount Browne for weeks now. She's not there."

Jon's stomach dropped.

26

"You're sure they have no idea where Kate is?" Jon asked, as a feeling of nausea settled over him. Right now, he didn't care about Seth, and had sent him on his way with a warning not to leave the area.

Besides, he felt reasonably sure that he had nothing to do with Harper's death, and that this Tiana would provide him with an alibi. He could tell from Seth's body language and how he'd been talking that he'd had the weight of the world on his shoulders and desperately needed to get rid of it.

But no, all he cared about right at the moment was finding Kate.

"Nope. She's not at Mount Browne, and she was never summoned there," Nathan replied.

"I have a really bad feeling about this," Jon said as he strode into the office and round to the incident room. He turned the lights on, and the whole case was laid out before him on the whiteboard, complete with photos of the first three victims. He'd not seen the board since Emily Murphy had been added to it, and seeing all three of them on there together, he felt something click. A link. A connection between all three that was just out of reach.

As Jon stood there, staring at the dead women's faces, he could imagine a fourth photo getting added to the board. The idea of seeing Kate's face up there, staring out at him and accusing him of letting her down, filled him with dread. He remembered the photos back in her apartment, her smiling face beaming out of them. He'd had a similar feeling back then too.

As he looked again at the corpses, especially Emily's, his mind was suddenly filled with images and memories of Charlotte, dead in their home. She'd been murdered by a killer that had taken an interest in him, and he had a terrible feeling that history was about to repeat itself.

He couldn't allow that. He couldn't let someone else he liked die on his watch. The thought of Kate being killed by this guy made him want to throw up and punch his way through the next wall at the same time.

This was why he'd avoided close relationships with anyone since Charlotte. The idea of losing someone else to one of these psychopaths, he felt like that might actually break him.

He couldn't let her down. He had to find her. He had to push his rage and fear to one side and concentrate on doing his job and finding her before it was too late.

"It's him," Nathan replied. "It's Abban. I know it."

"Abban?" Jon asked, a little perplexed, but then as he thought about it, maybe that wasn't such a crazy idea. "Okay, I mean, I get it, he hates her and wants her dead, but how does that fit into these murders?"

Nathan frowned. "It wouldn't. Why would it fit into this case? They're two totally separate things. Abban has hated Kate since forever, but that has nothing to do with this killer," Nathan replied, waving at the board.

"No," Jon replied as the idea gripped him ever more fiercely. This felt right. This was the link. "You're wrong. There's a connection here, I know it," he replied as he stared at the board. "This is *all* linked."

"Linked? I'm not sure about that."

"No, this is right, I know it. There's something about them," he said, pointing at the victims looking over at Nathan. "I know it."

"You know it? So we're going on a hunch now?"

"I don't know… maybe…" Jon replied, and as he turned back, he thought the board was filled with pictures of Kate for a moment. Three images of her face staring out at him, and three shots of her dead, murdered body.

But it wasn't. It was the three victims, and yet, the link between them and Kate suddenly got closer. If he could just somehow make that connection between them and Kate, it would all just slot into place. It felt so tantalizingly close.

It was right there.

He went through it again in his head. Three victims. All of them female, all young women, all with their fingers cut off, all three with...

"No," Jon stiffened, his eyes darting back between the three girls.

"What? What is it?" Nathan asked.

"Shit, of course. Why didn't I see it before?"

"See what?"

"Look, look at them. Shit, that's not a good photo of Mollie. That's not up to date. But still, look. What's the same?"

"Well, there are a few things..."

"Imagine Kate's photo up there. What do these three have in common with her?"

"But, they don't... Oh, no. Oh shit."

"You see it?"

"The hair. They all have auburn hair."

"And so does Kate," Jon replied. "I mean, that's not a good headshot of Mollie, she changed her hair since then, but you can see her hair colour in the crime scene images."

"So, this is all to do with Kate?" Nathan asked.

"It has to be."

"But what about everything else? The killings and the fingers?"

Jon stared at the photos of the crime scenes, thinking back to the derelict factory where they found Harper, and then the tree where Mollie had been killed.

As he thought back to Emily and how she'd been strung up, he knew it wasn't entirely about Kate. It was about him and his past too. This was about both of them. The victim, Emily, still looked like Kate, though.

But if the Marionette scene was about him, then the other two had meaning also, but their meaning was for Kate, not him.

And then it clicked.

"Of course! Look. This one, Emily, it's a case from my past. It's clearly a copy of the Doll Killer case I worked on. Then look here, Mollie was tied to a tree, like the first killing that Wilson Hollins did."

"Damn, yeah. Kate's first case with us."

"Yes," Jon replied, seeing Nathan's expression change as he started to get it.

"Shit, and Harper, she was killed in a derelict factory, which is like Kate's second major case with us."

"Solomon Lichwood," Jon said, remembering the name that Kate had told him the night before.

"That's right. So, how does this help us?"

"They're all important cases from our past," Jon said.

"But, if that's what he's doing, how do we know what's coming next?"

"They're going back in time," Jon replied as he looked at the order again.

"They're what?"

"The killings, look. The derelict factory, Harper, was first. Then Mollie and the tree was next, which goes back earlier to Wilson. Then the Marionette relates to me and the Doll Killer."

"Which was when?"

"Five years ago," Jon replied. "So the one before that was..."

"Fiona," Nathan replied.

"The Stone Circle," Jon agreed. It all fit. It must be right.

"You know about that?" Nathan sounded curious.

Jon nodded. "She told me last night."

"Oh... I see."

Jon shrugged as Nathan shook his head, banishing that train of thought.

"But wait," Nathan said. "Solomon wasn't Kate's most recent case, that was the Abban case, so why would this killer start with Solomon?"

"I think the killer is connected to Abban somehow," Jon replied. "It has to be, and if it is, then he's clearly just looking at cases that happened before he got caught and ignoring his own."

Nathan pulled a face. "Abban? Why do you think it's Abban? There's no link between him and the killings... Oh, shit, no. Of course!" Nathan slammed the base of his first against the nearby table and groaned in frustration. "Why didn't I see it?"

"See what?"

"The connection to Abban. It's obvious."

"Is it?"

"The fingers," Nathan replied. "When we moved in to arrest him, he got shot and lost two fingers on his right hand. Goddamnit, why didn't I see that?"

Jon's mind raced as he started to fit it all together. He suddenly remembered Abban's wife, Faye, and how she held up her hand in the V-for-Victory sign, mimicking the injury her husband had. Hell, she'd thrust her hand into Jon's face making that sign. She'd shown him the clue early on.

He'd thought she was just hoping to win the case, but there was more meaning to it than that.

"So, he mimicking our cases, killing young women who look like Kate with auburn hair, cutting their fingers off to mimic what happened to him, and the cuffs just signify the police."

"Makes sense," Nathan replied.

"But if we're right, how'd he do it? He's been in custody, under lock and key. The only thing I can think of is..."

"He had help. Help who sprung him from custody while he was in transit," Nathan replied, fishing his phone from his pocket and waking it up. "Listen to this, 'Police suspect Abban had outside help who crashed into the van and freed him.' Alright, so that's how he did it. Then, if Fiona's case is next, maybe he's going to kill Kate at a stone circle?" Nathan suggested and then darted out of the incident room, making for his computer as Jon followed, full of nervous energy.

"We need to find a stone circle that's close by," Jon suggested.

"Way ahead of you," Nathan replied as he dropped into his seat and started hunting. He pulled up a search engine and started going through links.

"What's that one?" Jon asked, peering at the unclear thumbnail image.

"Hascombe Hill," Nathan replied, clicking into the Wikipedia entry for it, and then enlarging one of the photos.

The image revealed a mist-wreathed countryside with a circle of large standing stones on a hill, while bare, wintery trees stood stark against the morning sky.

"That's it," Jon said. "She's there. I know it."

"There might be others."

"No way, she's there."

Nathan nodded. "Yeah, I think you're right, but I also think we're on our own."

Jon nodded. They needed to go now. If they delayed, Kate could die, and he would do everything in his power to keep that from happening. Justifying backup might be tricky too, given this was just a hunch, but he felt confident they could get at least one car on their way down there.

"Alright, let's go."

27

"Tell them no lights or siren," Nathan suggested.

Jon nodded. They needed the element of surprise. Looking into his side mirror, Jon saw the patrol car behind them. "No blues and twos, alright?"

"Sir," the officer in the car replied.

Jon nodded and ended the call before his phone suddenly buzzed again. It was Rachel.

"Rach," Jon said, answering.

"They found her car," Rachel replied.

"Kate's?"

"Yeah, looks like it was rammed off the road. No sign of Kate though."

"Shit. Where are you?"

"I'm on my way to the Station, what can I do?"

"I'd like another car or two of backup ASAP, also an ambulance, just in case—you never know. But they must not get there before us. We need to keep the element of surprise," Jon said.

"Okay, text me when you get there, and I'll make the calls."

"Excellent. Get the team in and brief them."

"Will do. And Jon?"

"Yeah."

"Bring her back alive, okay?"

"I will," Jon replied. "You have my word."

Rachel hung up and Jon stuffed his phone in his pocket.

"She was run off the road and kidnapped," Jon said.

"Damn it," Nathan replied, accelerating along the backroad through the early morning twilight. In the east, the sky began to lighten, turning orange, red, and purple as the sun got closer to rising.

"We're not crazy for thinking Abban is behind this, are we?" Jon asked.

"I don't think so," Nathan replied. "It all fits. I just hope we've chosen the right site."

"Are there lots of stone circles in Surrey?" Jon asked.

"I don't think so. Also, this one isn't old, it's only been there for about twenty or thirty years."

"Oh. Does that make a difference?"

Nathan shrugged. "No idea. I doubt it."

"Mmm, yeah. This is about taunting us, I guess," Jon replied, unable to stop the feelings of doubt that ran through his mind, along with the terrible guilt he felt. Was this somehow his fault? Had he somehow cursed Kate by working so closely with her? His mind couldn't stop making comparisons between this and Charlotte's murder, and wondering if somehow they were connected. Maybe they were barking up the wrong tree with this Abban thing, and it wasn't him at all. Could it be something to do with his own past? Was the Doll Killer out, and up to his usual tricks again?

It all seemed so surreal, like some kind of living nightmare that he couldn't wake up from.

"So, when did Kate tell you about Wilson and Solomon?"

Jon did his best to keep his face neutral but struggled to keep any kind of grimace off his face entirely. He'd wondered if Nathan would end up talking to him again when he found out about them going on another date.

Little did he realise how far things had gone, last night.

"We went for another drink last night after we found Emily's body."

Nathan sighed. "Yeah. Damon told me about the Doll Killer. Sorry about your girlfriend."

Jon nodded, feeling awkward. "Thanks."

"I didn't know."

"I didn't expect you to. It was a long time ago, and I'm over it for the most part."

"Yeah. Those moments aren't easily forgotten."

"Nope."

"I think I would've needed a drink too if I were in your shoes," Nathan said. "I hope Kate was able to... help in some way?"

"She did," Jon replied. "Hopefully, I can return the favour now. I don't want to lose anyone else."

Nathan nodded. "Me neither. I'm with you all the way."

"Thanks, man."

"No problem. Anytime."

"Do you think we'll find her?"

"Hope springs eternal," Nathan answered before he looked over. "We'll find her."

Jon nodded, and for the next few moments, they sat in silence as Nathan navigated the roads through the countryside south of Guildford, making for the Hascombe Stone Circle.

"Look, up there," Nathan said, pointing out his driver's side window. Jon leaned down to look. He could see some flickering light, and what looked like tiny dark dots on the side of the hill.

"That's it, isn't it?" Jon remarked, staring at the lights. They looked like flames from their colour and how the light seemed to dance in the half-light. "Do we stop here?"

"No, I think I can get closer."

"Hurry up," Jon said and kept his eyes on the target as Nathan continued up the road, past the hill, before turning right. Heading up, Nathan drove along a back road that angled back towards the monument.

Eventually, on their right, Jon spotted a barn that looked like it was owned by some kind of business. There was a small gravel car park outside with a lone white van occupying it. Nathen pulled in, skidding to a stop.

Finishing up his text to Rachel, Jon jumped out and moved to the boot, pulling out a stab vest. Donning it as quickly as he could, he looked over at the van and noted the churned up gravel at the back of it, and pulled a face. It suggested a scuffle by several people, perhaps as they forced Kate out of the back of the van, over the fence, and up the hill to the stone circle. Jon shivered, there was just something about white vans that was incredibly creepy, and the thought of Kate in the back of it, possibly injured and terrified, chilled him to the core.

As he finished securing the vest, he looked over at Nathan and the two uniformed officers that had joined them.

"Ready?"

"Yep," Nathan nodded.

"Ready," one of the officers replied.

"Good. No heroics. Let us handle them, and you back us up."

"We'll follow your lead," the man answered.

"Excellent. Then, let's go," Jon replied.

He turned and moved to the nearby fence without another word, vaulting it, and making for the fields beyond the barn. Hopefully, the building had hidden their approach, and they retained the element of surprise.

Out here, away from the streetlights, it was still quite dark, even with the growing light in the sky. The clouds were shot through with crimson and tangerine that faded to indigos the further away from the rising sun it got. It was both beautiful and ominous.

The kind of sunrise that a photographer like Kate would love to try to capture.

Ahead, beyond several lone trees and a couple of bushes, he could see the flickering light of flames. As they ran in silence, coming out from behind the last overgrown bush, the stones came into view. They stood proud on the hill, silent monoliths watching over the surrounding countryside without passing judgement.

Within the circle, two campfires had been lit on either side of the central stone. The glow from those fires lit the three figures inside the circle, and the scene made Jon feel sick to his stomach.

Two of them stood, facing the third who had been bound to the central standing stone by ropes so that she faced the rising sun. He could see the familiar ponytail that Kate always wore and knew it was her.

Jon put on a final sprint, pushing as hard as he could to reach the circle, and as they approached, it became clear that they'd been spotted.

The men turned to face Jon, the light from the fire and the sky catching their faces, revealing them. He recognised both. Abban stood closer, a couple of metres in front of Kate, his hands behind his back, watching calmly as Jon drew closer. The other man was younger and stood beside Kate, holding a huge pair of bolt cutters. The jaws of the cutters gripped Kate's little finger as he sneered at Jon. It took Jon a moment to place who he was and then he recognised him.

"Brendan," Jon muttered and saw Kate look up.

"Jon… Nathan…" she croaked weakly.

"Shut it, you," Brendan hissed, twisting the cutters and making Kate wince.

"Indeed," Abban replied. "Like father, like son. Nice of you to join us for our little ceremony, Jon. I did wonder if you might work it out before we finished here today. And you, Nathan."

"Wouldn't miss it for the world," Nathan replied sarcastically.

"I really did think you would work it out a *little* earlier," Abban continued, before raising his right hand. Jon could clearly make out the missing two fingers on Abban's right hand, leaving just his forefinger and middle finger which he held in a V shape.

"We worked it out early enough," Jon replied.

"Not really, Jon. You have three promising young ladies' deaths on your conscience now, all because you couldn't work out my frankly obvious clues."

"My conscience? Hardly. I wasn't the one who slaughtered them and watched them bleed out."

"No," Abban agreed with a smile and a look of pride. He glanced back at Brendan. "That is true, and I couldn't be more proud."

Jon took a step forward.

Brendan shifted, lifting the bolt cutters. "A-ah, no you don't."

Kate hissed in pain and whimpered.

"Oh, I do love that sound, don't you?" Abban said, looking back to Jon. "That helpless, pained sound that women make when you hold their life in your hands. They plead with you, offering anything in exchange for their life. They'll let you do anything to them if you'll just let them live. It's so exquisite, so choice, don't you think?"

"I have no idea what you're talking about, you sick fuck," Jon grunted. "Now *you* shut up, and let me tell you how this is going to play out." He looked over at Brendan. "Son, you're going to lay down those cutters and move away from her, and then you're going to get down on your knees."

Looking to his right, Jon could see the two uniformed officers had their Tasers out and ready. He caught the eye of one of them and waved him to wait. If Abban got hit first, or they shot Brendan, he could take off Kate's finger in a heartbeat.

"Jon. You're new around here," Abban replied, "and I don't expect you to fully understand things. Plus, you're a northerner, which tells me quite a lot about you, but you're not in a position to order us around. You need to know your place, frankly."

"Don't be such a jerk, Abban, there's no winning this. You can't escape," Jon replied taking another step forward.

"Don't you come any closer or I'll do it! I'll cut her finger off," Brendan warned.

"Do it," Kate urged. "I don't care."

"Quiet," Brendan shouted and kicked Kate in the gut. Jon winced, hissing through this teeth to see her in such pain.

"What do you want?" Jon asked, wanting to keep him talking. "Why do this?"

"It's none of your business, frankly," Abban replied. "This is between Kate and me."

"Fiona," Jon muttered.

"Oh, so you know? Well then, maybe that changes things. Yes, I suppose that comes into it a little. You see, I've relished tormenting little Kate here from afar for years. It's been a nice little distraction when I'm bored. But I did make her a solemn promise, one that I always intended to keep. Do you know what that promise was, Jon? How about you, Nathan?"

"You said you'd show her what a real killer can do," Nathan replied.

"Correct," Abban replied, as Jon inched slowly closer. He kept his movements slow and non-threatening hoping to get just a little closer to them, but mainly to Brendan, hoping to stop him from hurting Kate.

"Now, isn't that interesting," Abban continued. "Kate trusted you with that piece of information, Nathan, but not you, Jon. Hmm, makes you wonder, doesn't it?"

"Not really," Jon replied. What was his game, why was he talking like this? Normally they didn't want to talk, but Abban here actually seemed like it's exactly what he wanted. It felt like he was stalling for time. "I've only known her for a few days."

"But you did go on a nice date with our dear sweet Kate last night, didn't you? You ended up going back to hers, as well, for some alone time, right? Was she good? Did she please you, Jon?"

"That's none of your business, sicko."

"Oh, come on. I think it's very much my business. I've made Kate's business my business for a long time now. Besides, I think Nathan here might be interested in your womanising ways when it concerns our darling Kate."

"Womanising ways? What are you talking about?" Jon replied, flustered. Abban was playing divide and conquer. Did he expect to make Nathan turn on him? "She invited me…" Jon added as he glanced right. He could see the anger in Nathan's eyes as he stared at Abban.

Nathan glanced at Jon, meeting his gaze before looking back at Abban.

Jon couldn't read anything in those eyes and wasn't sure how this might turn out. Was it working? Would Nathan's protective instinct towards Kate make him turn on him?

It all felt like it was on a knife-edge as if it could tip either way, and all it would take would be just one little push.

"Don't listen to him," Jon muttered towards Nathan.

"Ignore him," Kate added.

"Shut up, the lot of you," Nathan growled.

"Oh, this is too delicious," Abban replied, grinning like a Hyena. A cloud swept away from the sun, and light broke over the horizon, splashing over the stones.

Abban's smile turned cruel. "Now."

Brendan tensed, closing the cutters and Kate screamed.

Turning, Abban raised his hand, brandishing a knife, and lunged at Kate.

Jon broke into a sprint.

Tasers popped and buzzed, but hit nothing.

Dropping the cutters, Brendan tackled Jon. Kate's scream became animalistic. Nathan charged past, and Abban shouted.

Jon landed on the ground with Brendan atop him, his face was rage and fury. Spittle flew as Brendan went for his neck and then punched him.

Seeing stars, there was a blur of black, and Brendan's weight was suddenly relieved. Coughing, Jon rolled over, catching his breath. Grunts and frantic shuffles to Jon's right forced him up. With a shake of his head, Jon got to his feet to see Brendan wailing on his uniformed colleague, outclassing him, and turning his face into a bloody mess.

Glancing right, Kate was still tied to the stone with a knife embedded in her upper left chest, hissing and writhing in pain. Beyond her, Nathan chased Abban into the morning sun, followed by the other officer.

Focusing on Brendan, Jon gritted his teeth and pulled his baton. Extending it with a flick of his wrist, he stalked towards the fight and then rushed in, shoulder barging Brendan. The man grunted as he fell, but rolling to his feet.

"You bastard," Brendan cursed.

"Do you talk to your mother like that?"

Brendan roared and rushed him. Dodging right, Jon swung the baton and caught him on the side. The uniformed officer rushed him and slammed into Brendan, dropping him to the ground where they rolled.

"Get off me!" Brendan shouted.

He kicked, throwing the officer off of him, and started to rise as Jon rushed in.

Jon knocked Brendan back. Falling, the younger man tripped and toppled over, landing in the flames of the nearby campfire. Brendan panicked and screamed as he tried to get out of it.

Jon hesitated, torn between helping him and letting him burn.

Brendan finally got out of the fire pit, but his clothes had caught fire. Flames licked up his torso and face. He dropped and rolled, wailing and whimpering until the flames went out. Rushing up to him, Jon held his nightstick ready and stood over him.

"Stay down."

Brendan's face was badly burnt, his skin black and cracked, his hands were a mess too. The killer stared up at Jon through hate-filled eyes, shaking with pain.

"I'll fucking kill you," he hissed as saliva bubbled and out of his mouth.

"Shut up," Jon said and grabbed him. Rolling him over, Jon pulled the man's hands behind his back and cuffed him. "You're under arrest for the murders of Harper Richards, Mollie Hayes, and Emily Murphy," he said and recited the police caution. The uniformed officer came to his side and put his knee on Brendan's back. His face a bloody mess.

"I've got him," the man said. "See to her."

Jon nodded once and rushed over to Kate. He could hear sirens and spotted flashing blue lights along the road at the bottom of the hill.

Rounding the central stone, Kate was still bound to it by ropes, her arms held out wide. The little finger on her left hand was missing, and the stump was bleeding badly. But more worrisome was the dagger she'd been stabbed with. It was embedded in her upper left chest, just below her collar bone.

Breathing hard through gritted teeth, her eyes watering, she looked up at Jon.

"Did… Did you get him?" she asked, struggling to speak.

"I got Brendan," Jon replied and looked off down the hill. "I don't know about Abban."

"You have to get him."

"We will. Don't worry, Nathan's on it. But I need to help you. Let me untie you."

"Okay," she grunted and winced with pain.

Carefully, Jon untied her right wrist and then her left. Kate gasped and clutched her injured hand as he went to work undoing the other ropes. As they loosened, she dropped into a sitting position.

"Oh god, it hurts so much," she said and looked down at the knife.

"I don't know if I should pull it out," Jon admitted. "I think we should leave it."

Kate nodded, her eyes closed tight, her face a mask of unrelenting pain.

Looking left, Jon made out blue lights parked up in the same car park they'd used, and what looked like figures running their way.

"Help's coming, just hold on, okay?"

Kate nodded.

"I'm sorry. I'm so sorry. This is all my fault."

"No, it's not," she replied, looking up at him. "You didn't do this."

"I'm cursed..." he muttered, ignoring her as thoughts of Charlotte appeared in his head. He should never have gotten so close to her. He brought this upon her.

"Don't be silly, This would have happened with or without you. Abban hates me, not you."

Jon sighed and nodded, but wasn't convinced.

"Sir?" Jon turned to see the paramedics rushing in. "Move aside sir, let us get to her."

Jon shuffled back and sat in the grass as he watched the paramedics go to work, setting up a stretcher and moving Kate onto it.

He shifted further back and felt something odd under his hand. Looking down, he saw Kate's finger in the grass, bloody and pale.

"Oh, shit. Hey, I've found her finger!" he called out, pointing to it.

"Where?" the paramedic asked and rushed over to collect it.

"Do you think you can put it back?"

"I don't know, we'll try," the man replied as they continued to work, before finally lifting her up on the stretcher and setting off down the hill. By now, a couple more officers had arrived, Brendan had been taken away, and as Jon looked around he spotted Nathan and the other officer leading Abban back up the hill towards the circle.

Abban looked furious.

"Not smiling anymore, are you?" Jon stated.

Abban spat at his feet, before being led off by uniforms.

"Kate's on her way to the hospital," Jon told Nathan who stood beside him as they watched Abban being led away.

"Good. I hope she'll be alright."

Jon nodded. "I'm sure she will be, and I hope you don't harbour any bad feeling towards Kate and me after…"

"Hey," he said, cutting in. "What you and Kate get up to is none of my business. I'm not her dad, and she's a grown woman. She can make her own choices."

"Yes, she can." Jon nodded. "So, you got him then?"

"Ah, yeah," Nathan replied. "With a little help. My legs aren't what they used to be."

"Amen to that," Jon replied, feeling the ache in his own joints. "Come on, let's go."

"I'm going to enjoy putting these two behind bars," Nathan commented as they walked down the hill.

"You and me both," Jon replied. "You and me both."

28

"Knock, knock."

Jon looked up to see Chief Superintendent Collins stood at his office door.

"Sir," Jon said.

"Good work today, Jon. You did well. You found your man and saved one of our officers. You should be proud."

Jon sat back and offered the chief a seat. "Thank you, sir. Although, Nathan deserves as much of the credit as I do."

"Don't worry, he'll get it. So, it was Abban and his son?"

"That's right. It was a campaign of terror aimed squarely at Kate and to a lesser degree, myself. As far as they were concerned, they were proving a point. This was all a sick power trip to them."

"So, nothing to do with Harper's gang contacts or the drug deals that Mollie and her friends made."

"Nope," Jon replied with a shake of his head.

"And Harper's missing father?"

"He got in touch today, this morning. He'd been on a camping trip in the Highlands and had no mobile signal. He's coming down to see Iris and talk to us."

"Good, good. So, how did Abban get Kate's number to call her this morning?"

"They got it from Francine, her neighbour. Turns out Brendan had been doing some handyman work for her to get access to her phone, and thus Kate's number."

"Jesus. That woman can't catch a break. She was the one that Abban kidnapped the first time around."

Jon nodded sadly, aware of this. "He knew she was a good target."

"Seems so. Okay, well, this all sounds like it's wrapping up nicely."

"Thank you, sir, it looks that way," Jon agreed. There were some side issues we could look into, such as Seth's gang contacts and the Millers, but that's a little beyond the scope of this case.

"Sure. So, what do you think? How have you found your first few days on the team?"

"Honestly, I'm tired and looking forward to a rest, but I like the team and have no plans to move back up north."

"I'm glad to hear it, Jon. I'm pleased to have you as part of this team. Keep me informed as to how things pan out, okay?"

"I will," he replied before the chief wished him a good day and left him to his work. The rest of the afternoon was taken up with reports, statements, and filing as they prepared for the interviews and got the case ready for court. But as the day wound to a close, Jon finally left the office and jumped into his car, making for Guildford.

Forty-five minutes later, after making his way through the evening traffic, he pulled into the Guildford Hospital car park and made his way up to the ward where Kate was recovering.

Walking into a room lined with beds, Jon spotted Kate easily, sitting up in bed, her arm held in an elevated position.

She turned and smiled as she spotted him walk in. "Hey," she said, her voice tired.

"Hi. How're you doing?"

"I'll survive. You're not getting rid of me that easily."

"Good," he replied with a smile. "How's your hand?"

"They reattached my finger, and they think it'll work fine. Might be a bit gammy but, I'll be okay."

"Glad to hear it. So, I was wondering, why your left hand and not your right, like the others?"

"Circumstances, I think. When you showed up, Brendan just grabbed the closest finger he could."

"Heh, yeah. Suppose that makes sense."

"So, we got them, right?"

Jon nodded. "We did. Abban and Brendan are in custody. We've already started on the interviews, and they'll probably be charged tomorrow. Then, it's in the hands of the courts. We even have footage from a camera in the transport van of Brendan freeing his dad."

"Good. Hopefully, they'll both spend the rest of their lives in prison."

"One can hope," Jon replied. "Look, I know you don't think this was my fault but—"

"But nothing, Jon. You didn't cause this. Abban would have done this regardless of who became our DCI. You're not to blame."

"Okay," he replied, but deep down he wasn't quite so confident. He knew it was silly, all this thought of being cursed, but he couldn't help it. A part of him couldn't let go of the idea that at some level, he'd been a part of what caused them to kidnap her.

"You need to let go of that guilt complex, Jon," Kate continued. "You really do. Charlotte's death and my kidnapping are not your fault. You need to stop tearing yourself apart over things beyond your control."

"I know." He sighed. "But I've been carrying this around with me for a while, and I don't think it will be that easy to stop. Also, I should have come with you. I might have been able to stop this from happening," he said, pointing to her hand. "I should have done better."

"Stop, Jon. Just stop. You can't think like that, it'll tear you apart."

"I guess," he replied reluctantly, staring at the floor.

"Look, Jon. I've been thinking, I need to talk to you."

"Oh?" He looked up, sensing this would be a serious conversation.

"Yeah. Look, I like you. I do, but I think we might have moved a little too quickly. You know?" She looked over at him earnestly.

"Oh, I see."

"I just think we need to cool things down a bit. What I did last night, I don't normally do that. I think I just need some time."

"I understand," Jon replied feeling his heart sink. He felt sad, and part of him wanted to fight her on it. He wanted to plead his case and get her to rethink things. But there was another part of him that actually agreed with her, but for different reasons.

He'd enjoyed their evening together, and enjoyed feeling that close to someone again, but his guilt over Kate getting kidnapped welcomed her choice and felt that slowing down was the right thing to do.

"I'm not saying never," she continued. "I'm just saying, not now, okay?"

"I get it."

She sighed. "I don't think you do. I think you're going to hold a grudge."

"No. Absolutely not." He took a breath. "Look, yeah, sure. I like you, I do. But that was just one night, you know? I'm a grown man and I'm more than capable of giving you some time. In fact, I think I kind of agree with you, actually. This has moved quite fast and I do wonder if we did the right thing. Also, you're an amazing detective and I wouldn't want to lose that. I need you on my team."

"You're sure?"

"One hundred percent. Besides, I wouldn't want to be on the SIU without Barry the Finger by my side," he replied with a smile.

Kate blinked, her eyebrows raising as she stared at him. "Oh God, is that a thing now?"

"Don't know. You'll have to come back to work to find out."

"I can't wait," she replied sarcastically.

"Atta' girl. I'll see you soon, alright?"

Jon stepped out of Kate's ward and headed outside into the fresh air, leaving the sterile confines of the hospital behind. He wasn't sure what the future held for him, or for Kate, but tomorrow was another day, and he was looking forward to seeing what it brought.

THE END

Book 2, **A Tangled Web**, is available here:
www.amazon.co.uk/dp/B08RY6QSYL/

Author Note

Thank you for reading this book. I hope you enjoyed the first book in this new series and will join me in book two soon.

I've enjoyed writing it and drawing on my own experiences as someone born and raised in Nottinghamshire, who then moved to Surrey for a job.

My move wasn't quite as exciting or as dangerous as Jon Pilgrim's was, but it should help inform this series going forward.

If you would like to learn more about Kate's past, you might want to pick up my DC O'Connell trilogy of books, which details Kate's first few cases as a detective on the Surrey Murder Team.

They're not essential reading for this series though, and it shouldn't mar your enjoyment of the DCI Pilgrim series in any way.

Thanks again, and I hope to see you enjoying book two soon.

Kindest Regards,
A L Fraine.

www.alfraineauthor.co.uk

Printed in Great Britain
by Amazon